ANDY ROWEN

POTTERY MAKING

outskirts
press

Pottery Making
All Rights Reserved.
Copyright © 2023 Andy Rowen
v2.0

This is a work of fiction. Names, characters, businesses, places, events, locales, and incidents are either the products of the author's imagination or used in a fictitious manner. Any resemblance to actual persons, living or dead, or actual events is purely coincidental.

The opinions expressed in this manuscript are solely the opinions of the author and do not represent the opinions or thoughts of the publisher. The author has represented and warranted full ownership and/or legal right to publish all the materials in this book.

This book may not be reproduced, transmitted, or stored in whole or in part by any means, including graphic, electronic, or mechanical without the express written consent of the publisher except in the case of brief quotations embodied in critical articles and reviews.

Outskirts Press, Inc.
http://www.outskirtspress.com

ISBN: 978-1-9772-6221-9

Cover Photo © 2023 www.gettyimages.com. All rights reserved - used with permission.

Outskirts Press and the "OP" logo are trademarks belonging to Outskirts Press, Inc.

PRINTED IN THE UNITED STATES OF AMERICA

Pottery Making

*P*ottery Making PM is code words for "Chinese Spy Craft." Pottery is made by combining naturally occurring raw materials, such as clay, earthen minerals and water and shaping them into forms. Once shaped, the clay body is fired in a kiln at high temperature about 1950 degrees Fahrenheit to 2700 degrees Fahrenheit. It becomes hardened and heat resistant. Some of these objects are functional and ornamental ceramic objects. To create symmetrical pottery, Potters use wheel throwing and slip casting to create multiples of one object.

The earliest pottery objects originated before the Neolithic period around 29,000 to 25,000 BC in the Czech Republic. Craft from China dates to 18,000 years unearthed in a cave in Hunan province, southern China during the Paleolithic hunter-gatherer's era.

The Chinese and Taiwanese people are united by one language Mandarin, similar characters and spoken word. The political systems are different. Taiwanese follow the democratic system, while the Mainland Chinese follow the single party, autocratic and communist doctrine. China has been changing dramatically and is focused on modernizing their military: Air, Naval, Space and Ground forces. Both countries believe that their joint destinies will someday result in unification. Mainland Chinese wants this to happen within a decade,

The Chinese Communist Party (CCP) strongly advocates for the physical unification to happen without firing a bullet or invading the island of Taiwan, formerly known as Formosa.

Pottery Maker, Jian Wu, is being developed to become an MSS- Secret Service agent. As a Cage fighter. Jian Wu is paying off his father's gambling debts to the Wop Tu Triad. His present goals are to win several cage fights. The Wop Tu Triad is positive that Jian Wu will win his fights and pay off his father's 50,000 Yuan debt. That is a large sum of money and needs focused approach as this is not an insignificant sum. Jian Wu has several hats, but he needs a clear vision for himself and the Party faithful. Failure is not an option.

As a student, Jian does not impress anyone.

Pottery Making

During the day, he is a "Missing-in-Action" student; dozing till the sun goes down. At night, he is "best in class" cage fighter. With luck, his father's debts will be paid off in two years or less. There is no exiting the Wop Tu Triad. If he is released from the Wop Tu, the other gangs will use him to fight for them. Wop Tu will have to destroy or remove him from the living world.

The Wu family lives north of the Dong River in South-Central China in the southern province of Guangzhou. In the 1980s, Deng Xiaoping became the premier party leader of the People's Republic of China (PRC).

Ms. Wu (Jian's Mother) worked at the Dongguan Bohai Furniture. She makes a decent living and stays out of trouble. The father: Mr. Wu has a steady blue collar worker job. He is a gambling addict. He borrows money from various sources to feed his addiction. This debt is a major burden on the family. As a result, the Wu family is unable to make ends meet.

Susie Wu, Jian's younger sister is impacted by the one child policy. She is moved to the Wong family house in the neighboring province of Guangzhou. Susie Wu becomes Susie Wong.

Susie is a precocious child and even with her location disruption, she does not miss a beat and advances rapidly in grade school. She jumps a few grades as she progresses through primary school.

Although three years younger to her biological brother: Jian Wu, she caught up with him in secondary school. Unmotivated by studies, Jian was street smart and had distinct street survival skills. Susie was different and in a class of her own. China does not believe in second chances. You win or lose. You work hard and hopefully get to the top in the skill that you are good at. The Chinese Communist Party nudges their Party faithful to make it to a place where they can serve the Party and their individual needs. PARTY First, individual Second!!!

Jian Wu's fighting skills put him in a select class of fighters. He could use his hands and feet as lethal weapons. He did not need additional weapons in combat. He was a one-man fighting machine.

"The Party needs me to be one of their top fighters. I need to be there to make a difference for the nation." Jian ponders. "There are plenty of fighters, but not all are in the top class that I belong to."

Jian Wu had serious fighting potential and was

going to be in an elite class with advanced coaching from the highly trained Ministry of State Security (MSS) school. As a secret service agent, the Chinese Communist Party (CCP) did not want to draw attention to Jian Wu until he transformed from street fighter, to combat cage fighter to Secret Service agent. The Communist Party had serious development plans for Jian Wu.

On the other hand, Susie Wong aka Susie Wu was a brainiac kid. She was in her head and had all the skills that were required in the combat arena. Susie was a neo-classical and highly trained fighter and technician in the art of combat. She had very good instruction from the MSS on modern fighting weapons: Drones, night weapons, and tactical field equipment. She had wide ranging exposure to weapons used by the World Powers, Europeans countries and other Asian leaders. Chemical, Nuclear, Biological and missile technology. Recently, she was given additional classes on satellite, advanced laser, and magnetic resonance weapons. She was trained by the best and could hold her own in close fighting and remote combat. Her language skills and ability to master all sorts of new combat techniques and languages made her critical to the Chinese development plan.

Her MSS handlers had plans for Susie too.

The Taiwanese Secret Service Agents were unaware of Susie Wong or her brother: Jian Wu. The CIA and the British secret service were also in the dark about these "low level agents" of the PRC.

"low-level" was a term used for fighters who had not been used in the theater and were being prepared for combat in the next 10 years or so.

"mid-level" was a term used for fighters who were being used in small scale operations and had the ability to be brought up to speed in rapid deployment scenarios.

"High-level" fighters were persons who had been trained and used in tactical and operational fights and were prepared for attacks in the South China sea and beyond.

The future was good and these fighters were trained to become the future fighters of the Chinese operational, tactical, and strategic advanced fighting arms.

China was making a declaration that the next decade and beyond, the People's Republic of China (PRC) would rule the world and overpower the other world powers with a very straight attitude that nothing is impossible for the PRC.

Taiwan will be just a footnote in that story.

Jian Wu's Training

The Jian Wu story began in the late nineteen eighties in Guangdong province, South China Jian Wu, lean muscular physique, was built for cage fighting. Black hair combed straight back. He grew up in the suburbs of the province's capital city of Canton. The Cantonese kids from the South of China dreamed about martial arts. It was known as the "Bruce Lee" effect.

Jian's father had a severe gambling addiction. He was appropriating money to feed his addiction. The Wop Tu and other Triads combined Mr. Wu's debts from other lenders. With usury interest of 10 percent, the total debt was a mind-blowing Yuan 50,000. The chance of Senior Wu paying off his debts was practically impossible.

"That was two years of salary," said the Chief to himself.

"Beating up Senior Wu will get us nothing! We will lose the goodwill of the people!!" The Triad team told the Chief.

"Let us use the Junior Wu."

"Is it a good idea to put bets on Jian and register him in multiple fights staggered around the Province?" The Chief queried. "Some fights need to be intelligently played for wins and few losses."

"We need to control the loss column. If Jian loses, all the money we invest in the young Wu will be wasted."

The fight team assented in unison. This was an untried technique for such a large amount of money and needed the Wop Tu to think outside the box. Maybe even think in another box. It is difficult to judge if Jian was made for the "rough and tumble" of ultimate cage fighting.

"We will have to test him in less competitive fights where his chances are better," the leader instructed his team.

"As he builds up his confidence, he will get a better sense of the ring."

"Get the word out, we need to make money on this fighter!!"

"Keep it quiet as we develop this fighter for the big City fights."

"One day he will be our Ace-in-the-hole" said the chief with his voice rising.

The decision was made to strategically use Jian in fights around the province. The more fights he won, the more money they made. He was an unknown fighter with heavy odds against him. They wanted to make money on "Jian's fights." While his handicap was high.

"Once he started winning, then this unknown fighter would become a known entity and the money would depend on the opponent." The fight team was sure that this would not be a simple matter.

Jian Wu picked up tips and tricks from watching other fighters and mentors. He learned from the ultimate fighters and their genre. His evolution as a street fighter qualified him to informal and formal street combats by age 15. The Wop Tu took Jian under their wing. He was going to be a "Wop Tu" fighter.

Initially, they hired a Brazilian "Capoeira" martial arts trainer who taught him several grips and handholds in ultimate fighting. Capoeira is a Brazilian standing martial art that uses kicks, dodges, and sweeps to stop an opponent in a self-defense setting.

Capoeira is a Brazilian art of fighting that

combines elements of martial arts, dance, acrobatics, music, and spirituality. For self-defense, Capoeira is an effective way to defend oneself against another unarmed opponent. Taking advantage of this training, he was able to counter the various tricks that the older fighters threw his way.

Once Jian's fights were analyzed and memorized, then improved, he would be unbeatable. The instructors studied Jian's unorthodox style. Jian's newcomer style of fighting had given him a sequence of bad moves from movies and other street fights. The muscle memory and sequences had to be "unlearned" and new techniques inserted to adjust his style and movement to a classical new age fighter. The techniques that the Brazilian trainer was going to incorporate into Jian's fight style were developed in the streets and Barrios of Rio De Janeiro, Brazil, and San Paolo.

Pay Off His Father's Debts

Jian knew that he was fighting for his family reputation and to save his father and mother from "loss of face" and "eternal shame." The Wop Tu was investing in Jian's ability to become a fighter in the Octagon. Money changed hands in ultimate fighting and betting and that would be a conduit for getting payoff from Jian's wins for his father's debts and more. It would be a long shot. But at least, it was a better approach to get their money back. Beating up Jian's father was not good for business and it would have a serious impact on the lending business in southern China.

Additionally, the Wop Tu procured a Wing Chun instructor to initiate Jian into the Ultimate Fighting sport. Jian needed better nutrition and body conditioning and quality instruction. This was possible with quality food and training in unorthodox units off the grid. All this cost money and Wop Tu would have to pay money to train Jian and we are talking about 100,000 Yuan and hopefully the multiplier effect would get them approximately 200,000 Yuan. This would erase all the debt and more.

If this panned out and he became a star fighter, they would be able to get back some of the additional money that they put on Jian's fights. Small fights would get him noticed, then medium level fights bring him some fame and finally the big network fights at the big towns or cities. That is where the big money is usually made and where the newbie fighters earn their reputation. The Wop Tu realized by Jian's third fight that they had a good fighter in him, and the potential to make money.

The Triads in Southern China and other parts of Asia had developed a forward-looking strategy. They did not believe in complex strategies, just hundreds of years of managing their resources and money sources. No inventing the wheel.

Spaced Out Strategy

The fighting area (Octagon) or Cage was a hard way to eke out a living and no fighter could have too many fights in a week or even a month. Fights had to be spaced out. Recovery from big fights was slow. It depended on the individual. Some of their trained fighters were good but did not heal fast enough from their fights especially if they were bloodied, bruised, and beaten. Typical fighters had approximately one to two fights a month. Rest of the time was spent to heal and train the fighter and get ready for the next fight. Food was essential, but the Chinese medicines and balms were used to cure the fighters and their souls to reduce the PTSD effects of massive blows to the body and head. Boxing was another sport where the continuous effects of blows to the front of the face, temples and different parts of the cranium led to accumulation of long-term effects and brain injury. American football was another dangerous sport that resulted in accumulated damage to the brain and internal organs.

There was limited shelf life to the underground fighters and the Wop Tu believed that Jian had about twenty medium fights and about twenty big fights in that body of his. He was 15 plus years and would exceed forty fights before his 17th birthday. This was an optimistic outlook, but there must be good strategy and luck as Jian moves around the towns and villages. One bad fight could set them back for several months, half a year or even a year. That is unacceptable.

"Can any person take this amount of punishment and still be competitive?" "Fighters have been burnt out before they reached twenty ultimate fights."

"The Wop Tu wanted him to be their prize fighter for a period of two years at least."

"He could then be their trainer or agent for new fighters in the years ahead." This was a longshot or as the big guys verbalized it in the industry "freaking longshot or moonshot."

"Too much is riding on this man."

They knew that Jian's movements in the ring were being studied, analyzed, and choreographed by other fighters and that would prove to be his downfall. Once his movements became predictable, it was likely that his probability of winning would go down. They moved him around various towns and villages, so that very few fighters and their fight managers would remember him. The Wop Tu wanted to win and the only way they could do that is to have fresh fighters in the circuit and fighters that could learn from their mistakes. Insertion of new fighters, "bait and switch" techniques kept the opposition guessing. They had a few fighters that looked like each other and could be used as decoys to position Jian for fights that were meaningful to the Wop Tu.

They would have to sacrifice a few fighters on the path to bring Jian to the top of the "southern title" and the prize money.. Keep the gamblers coming and betting. Keep the fighters trained to alter their formula and come out looking like new fighters, even though they were known entities.

The Triad and the Wop Tu tried to beat the odds. The Triad and Wop Tu always won the odds.

The fighters always lost part of their life in the ring. Their bodies were messed up and they proved to be of no value to the Triads in the long run. The Wop Tu would make a sacrifice of Jian when the time was right.

That time is coming and the Triad boss will

give the signal for the fight that Jian will go down for. Sometime before the Chinese New Year. Those fights were always critical. There were many drunken workers who would throw money as they were heading home to their villages for festivities.

Training

Jian Wu's Wing Chun instructor started to train him for the next several fights.

"You need to come to my training ring and get a few hours of training daily during your rest days and update your moves." said the instructor to Jian.

"I will be there every day, but I need to rest a bit between fights or I will be unable to lift my hands in the octagon." Jian replied.

"You are right, but you are becoming a creature of habit. Every time you enter the ring, you use the same set of starter moves." The instructor continued.

"The fighters are studying your moves and realizing how you repeat the same left, right strokes, so they parry your moves and come in real fast. Then they execute a set of counter moves that will get you in trouble."

"One of these days, Jian, your luck will run out." Strong fatalistic words from the instructor. Jian interrupted the instructor, "What should I do?

Pottery Making

What can I do? I have been successful so far. "Why should I change the winning formula?"

The instructor reached in and grabbed Jian with a head lock from the front.

"Stop getting used to the same formula." Instructor said.

"Predictability leads to blind spots and blind spots leads to losses and losses to deaths or broken limbs." intoned the instructor.

"Somebody will figure it out and come out with a new combination to beat you. Then you will be Pickle!! Or worse!!" said the instructor.

Jian was exasperated but was willing to adjust his fighting style and stance.

"I am all ears, just tell me what to do. What moves do I need to introduce into the next two or three fights.?"

Jian said, "How do I learn these new moves in a couple of days?"

"Take it easy. You need to absorb it slowly and make it part of your repertoire." Instructor chimed in.

"How does it become a part of my routine? And how do I develop my muscle memory?" asked Jian with less confidence.

The Instructor jabs him in the face without warning and as Jian jerked and starts to fall backward, He corrects himself and swings forward. This was expected and the instructor's knee was waiting for him. The knee if it made contact would be damaging to his face and would knock him unconscious. Jian slid past the knee and glided past the instructor's knee, heel.

As his head whisked by, he pivoted his head and used his hands to grab the instructor's foot. He applied pressure and tried to spin the instructor's body.

"Bad move, good intention!!"

The instructor countered with a massive one-two with his heel and a combination with hands and his other foot.

The blows were so fast and strong that it knocked Jian out. He pivoted off the two kicks and flipped to the floor face up. There was silence as Jian went to the ground. Fast breathing from the instructor, but no sound from Jian. He was out for the count or not…

However, he surfaced very quickly and rolled over. He was on his feet and coming at his instructor with an atypical move. He decided that this time he would not use his usual move sequence. Jian had seen enough. He needed to counter or come up with some of his own moves or he was toast.

The instructor feinted towards Jian's left and at the last minute came in fast with a one-two to Jian's head. Jian was very quick on his feet and his reflexes were very fast as he reacted instinctively to the trainer's sequence.

Jian learned his lesson and avoided a repeat. The next move would be his last, as the instructor came up rapidly with a smooth motion in a double scissor kick to Jian's unprotected head.

Jian saw the kick from a mile away but was unable to avoid the kicks to his head. He rolled away from the kicks and stumbled forward executing a similar set of heel kicks he had learned from his instructor. However, he failed to make contact to his instructor's head or body or legs and just kicked air.

The instructor used a Wing Chun move and just brushed Jian's legs away from his head and body with a stiff-arm deflection. The kicks were deflected and caused Jian to be unable to control his body's forward motion. This was getting very informative as the fight was turning out to be "move-counter, and counter kicks."

Jian continued to sway from side to side with motion forward, but constantly changing direction and letting the instructor come to him.

This unbalance led to his inability to right

himself, his motion took him forward and he fell sideways to the floor, rolled, and came back to face where his instructor should have been standing. This was a very smooth move, but the instructor was fast and had a lot of nimbleness in his footing and years of experience.

"Where is he? Has the Sifu disappeared?" Jian queried to nobody in particular.

The instructor was not to his right, left or in front of him.

He started to swear under his breath: "Where the hell is that mean son of a b…" he did not finish his sentence.

The shot that came from behind him was vicious and he felt the blow impact his shoulder and backbone, shuddering his total physical system. It was a knockout punch, but Jian was still standing barely.

He was vibrating and nearing a point of collapse. This could happen in any fight.

He swore at his instructor in rapid fire Cantonese, "Your father is a mean-spirited idiot and your mother is a whore." He continued, "Your sister had no business with the butcher's son for a few pieces of smelly meat."

The next two hits knocked him unconscious. He was lying on his back. Somebody threw water on his face and he came to. His instructor was calling the count. It was a technical knockout.

"Where am I? What happened?" Jian asked in a dazed voice.

"You called my family all sorts of scary names?" The instructor remarked.

"I was very scared and you definitely kicked the shit out of me." Jian intoned.

"That is what happens when you are over-confident. Confidence is good, but not when you are fighting without sufficient awareness and attitude." Instructor confessed.

"People have died from this bad attitude." The instructor continued.

"Yes sir!" "I learned my lesson. Thank you, xiexie ni."

"Thanks, and God bless you, my teacher!!" Jian bowed and groaned "Sifu" with profound respect in his voice.

(Sifu in Cantonese is a title for and role of a skillful person or master)

"I wish I could pay you. Unfortunately, I am not getting paid for my fights. Just food from the Wop Tu."

"Eventually, you will be paid for all you have learned and I will come knocking for money or favors."

"I promise to keep a running tally on the amounts I owe you. Will that be good enough?" Jian asked.

"That will be fine." The instructor replied.

"How is your social life? Are you tripping on alcohol? Drugs?"

"I don't have a social life!! Just family and a bunch of my male friends."

"The drugs and alcohol—I do not mess with that stuff."

"Women are tempting, but I do not know how to proceed, once I get into an affair or have an interaction with a lady."

"Now, Now, you must be interested in at least one fair maiden around campus?" asked the instructor.

"Yes, I have my eyes on this kind and beautiful lady but have not the slightest idea how to initiate contact." Said Jian, "Do you have any suggestions or ideas?"

The instructor was happy with this last bit of news, but his expression was bland and he did not show the internal happiness that he felt for Jian.

Teenage Hormones

Jian was aware of Helen Tsai around campus, but he was not sure about his intentions about the lady. He was not even sure if she would be interested in him. Too many questions were raging through his mind and he had no time to focus on what to do once he was face to face with her. The "Cage" was a known arena. He was familiar with the cage and ultimate fighting. "Women" are an unknown quantity. Women are difficult to understand "entity." Full of emotions, kind, loving and sometimes difficult to gauge. It was very tough for a fighter to treat a woman with kindness, love and sweetness. Jian would need to be reprogrammed to be able to respond to this new challenge. All the fights and years in the ground did not give him the slightest understanding of how to behave and respond to the women.

"What was going through Helen's mind." Jian pondered. "Would she be interested in me?"

"I need to be clear as to where her heart is?"

Jian would like to know all the beautiful thoughts racing through that pretty lady's mind.

"Secret love is fine, but one had to know and the only way is to tackle Helen and know her." Jian said to himself.

"Get close to her. I need to stop dreaming and corner this lady. One way or the other, I need to find out what are her thoughts and feelings about me." Jian continued.

In his line of work, he realized that thoughts like these would sink him. He had to continue to keep a clear and beautiful mind. Helen was secretly in love with Jian, but she also did have minimum understanding about love, affection, relationships and kissing a strapping guy like Jian.

She had heard on the grapevine that there were a few ladies who were attracted to Jian. He was known as a tough fighter and had won a few underground fights. That reputation was always exciting and got some of the ladies imagining all sorts of bad thoughts about Jian.

Helen was not in this "crazy head business". She was normal but inexperienced in the ways of the world. She wanted a stable man, but she did not have the slightest idea as how to corner a prize like Jian. Rumor around the school was that Jian was fighting for a reason and that reason was to settle family debts for the Wu family.

Helen did not know the extent of the debts or the amount of money that was at risk. She like most average people believed that the money was not high enough to warrant a lifetime of fights.

"He was probably fighting for an insignificant sum of money." She said to herself.

"Could someone fight forever?" She asked some of her friends

Same question she directed at her father.

Her Dad was non-committal, as he did not understand the fight business.

Helen said to herself, "I need to find this out by asking the devil (Jian) himself."

"I need a better picture of what is happening behind the curtains." She continued.

"He must love to fight with some unknown bad guys around the county."

"Jian will answer the fight question." She spoke to herself.

'There is no reason for him to not give her a reasonable reply."

"Right!!" Helen was obviously distraught about this matter.

Rumor has it that the other girls did not want to challenge her and stayed clear of Ms. Helen and Jian. That should have calmed Helen and Jian.

"Jian has the hots for Helen," murmured one of the guys.

"Helen does not know about him, but she will notice him soon." said his friend.

"How can we expedite this meeting?" the friend intoned.

"Jian is very aloof, and he seems distant when it comes to ladies," indicated the first speaker, " Maybe, somebody needs to light a fire under him."

"Not sure, if that will do it. It is very puzzling when a fighter stays away from the female crowd. That is great mighty discipline." The guys around him wondered.

"Someday the dam will break and Jian will fall in love with one of the ladies."

The speculation would not ebb.

Trouble in Paradise

Helen Tsai was compact in stature and aware that she and Jian had exchanged brief glances in the school halls. She was five foot six and her hair straight combed and well kept, not a hair strand out of place. Her eyes were average size, and her nice, rounded cheeks were smooth. Most Cantonese women were short in stature. She was the exception.

Her legs were athletic and sexy. Her toned body was lean and muscular, just proportionate to her body. Her mother did not approve of junk fast food, so Helen had no additional weight. Just toned muscle, well-proportioned arms, and legs. Helen's Mother had a very lean body too.

Helen was aware of the need to maintain good posture, good eating habits, and maintain a lean toned and muscular body. She was also aware of her image. She did not use makeup or lipstick or any of the cheap facial or body lotions. Her positive demeanor and her attitude towards the opposite sex, gave her an advantage over the other ladies in the class.

Helen maintained her grades in school and would make it to a decent southern college in China. Her attitude was very positive and friendly. She had poise, tact and managed her interactions with other persons at her school. Helen was headed for better things and her parents were attentive to her care, and development.

Her mother did not approve of her spending time with the "loser" kids. "Loser" kids was a technical term given to kids who were not getting any guidance from their parents and elders and had a tendency of meandering in their scholastic career and eventually in their later years. Her mother believed that Helen would do well in her school and later career and life. She was dedicated to her studies and participated in debates, intramural sports, and essential extra-curricular activities. She maintained a balance between her studies and her other activities. She was well rounded and maintained her grades.

In romance and dating, women did not make the first move, but she hoped that she would accidently bump into Jian. If not, our ancestors would position her strategically to make contact. The Chinese were not religious and did not believe in spiritual karmic or blind fate. They would have an altar filled with pictures of their ancestors at home or in the car and the older Chinese would follow the usual prayers to their ancestors which outsiders believed was some form of ritual to their deceased elders. It was very structured and not open to discussion. It was a private matter.

She investigated the Wu family. This gave her plenty of background information about Jian. She had some trepidation about his regular cage bouts, and she wanted to know more about him before she ventured into a relationship with him. The Cage fights were not a good place to be, and Jian had special personal reasons for participating in this risky sport. She assumed it was how boys matured into men. Risks were part of the young man's life and obviously she should not be interfering in his choices or personal decisions. There was time after she got to know him. He was old enough make mature decisions. No reason to kick up a storm, she hardly knew Jian or the Wu family.

She was impressed by the person and believed there was more to Jian than meets the eye. There was deep affection welling in her chest and she felt like love throbbing in her mind, heart, and body.

"Was this puppy love?" or "just infatuation"

"I love the way he moves and acts like these silent types" she pondered aloud.

"Maybe I need to make the first move!!" she added.

"I need to take the initiative. Why not, times are a-changing, and women could make the first move." She continued.

Helen was starting to beat the timeless drum about making the first move. She had not been trained or tutored in the mysteries of love and affection. This was her first time and her heart was beating fast.

"What if he does not reciprocate? What if he just walks away?" Her troubled mind puttered on.

"Jian would be a great protector, but his crazy interest in combat and cage fighting would get him into trouble with the authorities." She continued.

"It is worth a try." She added in haste.

"I must at least try to get in the ring and attempt to love this rascal."

She had no idea that he would leave the area sooner rather than later. She would have to stage an accidental meeting through friends she knew.

"Library and study rooms were out!! "Jian had no interest in his studies, "library, or any of the interesting places that girls like to hang out and meet their friends."

Pottery Making

"Think! Think!" Helen was worried. This internal monologue was driving her crazy, and her mind needed a quick and clean solution.

"I can't ask any of my girl buddies, they are a jealous lot!! They would steal him or destroy the possibility of us developing a relationship."

Helen pondered all her options, when suddenly out of the blue, she sighted Jian ambling around the corner and heading towards her general location. He had not seen her. She was in the shade of the building and sort of in the dark shadow zone. He was looking in her general direction, but he had not spotted her yet. That was not a problem. Soon their eyes would meet. He was cool and looking unperturbed.

She intended to wave at him. He seemed calm and collected. She glanced over her shoulder. No one within hearing range. Not a soul in sight.

"The luck of my forefathers and ancestors is shining on me today." Helen mouthed under her breath.

Jian was humming a local fight song or was it a love song.

Helen to herself: "This is now or never."

She called out to him in a very mild and gentle voice: "Mr. Wu??" There was trembling in her voice and some hesitancy. The "Wu" sounded like "Woo."

Jian broke his stride and almost tripped as he realized who was calling his name. The rest of their conversation just came out rapidly. Jian's heart was racing.

"I have been meaning to talk to you. And its Jian not Mr. Wu…" Jian said.

He was nervous and his words were tumbling out. He was flustered.

"OK. Mr. Jian, my name is Helen, and I am happy to meet you."

"Let us skip the Mr., If its Ok with you, let us just use JIAN." He said very slowly, spelling out his name like she was an idiot.

Of course, she knew how to spell his name and probably the name of everyone in the school.

Jian looked around and realized that they were alone. He wanted to grab her sweet face and kiss it not once but multiple times. He had never kissed a woman and he had no idea of how to do it. There was no instruction manual.

In south China, kissing in public even with close family was scorned. His face was turning red. He was really getting bent out of shape. This was crazy. He was breathing hard and talking fast like he had a race to run.

"Slow down, Slow down, buddy…" he muttered under his breath.

"Did you say something?" Helen probed.

"No, No I was just talking to myself" Jian apologized.

Helen was having the shakes and she was about to wet herself with all the crazy thoughts shuttling through her mind. Her legs were trembling and her heart was beating at a rapid rate.

"Slow down!!" Helen said under her breath.

"This man is really sending all these energy waves in my direction."

"I am about to collapse under the strain of just talking to him." Helen said.

"This was really crazy and we have not even touched each other." She continued.

"What is wrong with me?" Helen said.

" What will happen if he leans in and kisses me." Helen continued.

She was hoping that Jian would lean towards her and cut the distance between them from twelve inches to a few centimeters and just brush her cheeks or more boldly her lips with his own. She would have fainted with the proximity of their aerial love making.

This was just a fleeting thought and she could see that Jian was also shaking with all the excitement and energy passing between them. Her eyes met his and it was like they knew each other from the time they were born. "They were soulmates."

"We need to continue onward or I will fall down in the quad." Helen was in agony. If ever this became something more than a first stranger meeting, Helen was sure that she and Jian would be in a tight embrace.

They parted company, never holding hands or making any major moves but just simply "getting to know each other" stuff.

Helen was happy with the outcome. But she needed to use a restroom and soon. She needed to wipe the sweat off her face and the back of her neck which had gone hot. Her heart was beating and I am sure Jian could hear her heart as well as his own. The trickle that was going down her back was too much for even Helen.

That was the first meeting. More would come later. If there was a later.

She practically ran into the restroom and reached into her bag to get a tissue out and spilled the contents of her bag on the floor. She was a mess.

Helen barely slept that night. She felt something deep in her soul.

"Was it love or just a blind attraction?" She had

to talk to her mom or some adult. She needed an adult opinion on a sensitive matter.

Just state the facts and tell her mom what happened. Mother will know how to take it from there.

The Tsai family was a quiet and simple family that was not used to histrionics and unwanted drama. Mother was very active with the townspeople and she was very charming with the neighbors and the older folks.

The Father was molded in the southern stoic Cantonese style of living. He reported to work and was able to make a decent amount of money. No bad habits, smoking, gambling, or chewing any kind of mind-altering drugs. His simple lifestyle and his wife's kindness and demeanor had helped in the neighborhood. They were an up-and-coming family with some expectations for their daughter. Helen was quite competent and they expected that she would do well in her career.

Helen had learned some behaviors from her mother and some from her father. At school, she was a "middle of the road" child and although she was not extremely bright, she was in the top 50 percent of the class. The other girls in her classes were enamored by her attitude and were willing to join her in small harmless adventures around the school.

Late night activities were not her thing and she did not approve of any boy-girl attractions, tomfoolery, and public displays of affection. It was unbecoming of the persons and Chinese society although modernizing did not look kindly on that type of activity.

She did broach the "affection" topic with her mother when father was not present. She started to introduce her mother to the "Jian" episode and "how she felt about Jian."

Mother was not shocked but was liking the fact that her daughter was seeking her advice about love and relationship. "This was a good start."

To say that Helen was excited about her meeting with Jian is an understatement. She was falling for the brigand. She started to daydream and have dreams about Jian and her falling in love with him. This was not a good direction for her. She could see her life evolving with Jian and that they would have at least one child, a boy or two… "kids why not more children."

"need to calm down, little cat girl," she said to herself as she looked in the mirror. "What am I getting all flustered about?"

"This Jian is my flesh and blood, not a complete stranger," said Helen.

"We are not even making physical contact and I am acting like a total idiot." She continued, "Jian was a bit shocked and he appeared to take it in stride."

Helen needed a proper strategy to make this infatuation or minor love affair progress.

"I need to talk to my best friends."

" and some of my close relatives." Helen said to herself.

"I need to evolve this love story and need to speed up and

we would need to get married or get hitched quickly." Helen had some racing thoughts.

"The dynamics of marriage had evolved from the 1960s and 1970s." mused Helen. "Present day, in China, which was still socially backward."

"We are still controlled socially from the center. There were advances in technology, social engineering websites, and advanced dating websites. However, we are traditional on the social aspect of life. The social fabric of the Cantonese people from south China allowed adults to select their own partners without interference from others."

"However, the 20 to 30% of individuals who were shy, backward, and not able to advance their own individual agendas were unable to express themselves in the public internet or dating space.

These persons were slow to adapt to the modern dating environment. If they did not visit social sites and worked at home without access to a computer, they were unable to find their online mates."

This was unfortunately the case with Helen Tsai, who was of the younger generation. China would adopt these social advancements in the next 20 to 30 years with incomes rising, women in the work force and with more Chinese students visiting other countries.

The social fabric was changing ever so slowly and the dating scene would advance eventually. The Chinese did not believe in following their Western brethren. Sexual promiscuity and activities like masturbation, gay, and anal sex were taboo and attributed to Western countries. The Chinese were not strangers to prostitution and harmless necking and petting between the opposite sexes.

The Northern Chinese or Han community were generally very conservative and maintained a tough posture towards loose morals and reckless sex. Punishments were severe and the Party did not believe in allowing their populations to venture into gay activities and HIV spread. The Chinese from the south and the coastal areas had some degree of freedom and behavior flexibility that allowed them to be able to resort to borderline activities like gambling, minor alcohol consumption, hashish, or minor drug smoking. Hard drugs like heroin and cocaine, were not so common. Guns and bombs were mostly inaccessible and the police and party would come down real hard on this activity.

The South China area would advance culturally and be more progressive like the Taiwanese and the West, while the Han people of the North would stay more conventional and conservative. Western China was remote and quite complicated by ethnic diversity, religion and people who spoke languages that sounded foreign to Mandarin, Cantonese, and other languages of the East Coast. The culture was different and had not changed since the days of Marco Polo and the silk road travails.

The Odds & The Fight

Jian Wu had several fights during his 15th and 16th years. He was getting better at the approach; his preparation and his mastery of the various techniques prepared him for the mediocre fighters he came up against. His confidence level and his ability to "think on his feet" and adjust his jabs, combination of moves and various adjustments as his body was getting bruised in some of the bigger fights.

The Wop Tu was happy as the money flowed into their coffers. They kept on healing their fighter and prepping him for the next fight. The 30th fight was in northern district of Guangzhou and there were accomplished fighters in that area. Many of these fighters were ex-Shaolin masters who had left the family and were fighting for money in the underground.

These blacklisted Shaolin Masters were very dangerous and posed a life threat to Jian Wu.

Pottery Making

The last two fights were in January and would involve two characters who used heavy vitriol and bad language before the fight and during the fight. This intimidation technique did not work with all opponents, but was used to demoralize the opponents and then attack savagely with combination hits and kicks to the groin and weaker parts of the body.

The Shaolin Masters were nicknamed as Shaolin J and the second was nicknamed Shaolin D for Death.

Shaolin J jumped all over the place and imitated monkey hops and tripped around the cage. However, Jian applied a series of masterful hits and combined to use a two fisted vice grip that made contact to both temples at the same time. J did not know what happened. He was jarred so badly that he came back and received the same hits twice. He went down and did not come back for more punishment.

The following week in the last week of January he advanced to the Shaolin D fighter. This D guy used all the techniques in his toolbox, screaming obscenities and calling Jian, his coach and family all sorts of names, he came across the floor and stopped just short of making contact, then pivoted and applied a sequence of heel kicks, hand blows followed by more monkey hops and silence. Mr. Jian waited for the opportune time and as D came at him with a lot of momentum and swinging at his head. He waited and met the guy in mid stride, he was airborne and hit him with twice the force.

The kicks and back handed fist hammer hits knocked the air out of the combatant. He went down and did not come up. That was end of Shaolin D.

THE KILLER K FIGHT

The Odds were against Jian for the Sunday knockdown fight with Killer K.

They were high odds and stacked against Jian Wu.

Jian Wu dead: 200 to 1

Jian Wu maimed: 100 to 1

Jian Wu in a coma: 50 to 1

Jian Wu to win: 1 to 10. Low probability.

Killer K was a tough fighter and had won every fight in the last two years. The persons who came against him were maimed and in most cases dead or barely able to move or breathe. Killer K was the cripple creator. He believed in taking the guys down. He did not believe in repeat fights.

Jian Wu was not expected to even survive this fight, so the Triad chiefs of Wop Tu were sure that he would not live to tell his side of the story. They had bet heavily on Killer K. The odds favored K and not Jian. A very small group had bet for Jian to win.

The previous two fights were arranged by Wop Tu to get rid of Jian. He had paid back his father's gambling debts and more, but he was becoming a burden to the Triad, and they needed to get rid of him "the easy way" in the octagon. Nobody left the Triads alive. The plan was to win some money as they eliminate Jian from the fight market. Jian was turning seventeen after the annual China New Year Holiday.

The last two fights in December and January were close fights and Jian was not expected to win them. However, his training and his mind control just got him over the top and he had two technical knockouts against very strong fighters.

They underestimated the trained street fighter. Jian would make them repent for their negative attitude towards him. They had lost some money, but not a lot.

"Who said that gangsters were a smart bunch?"

The MSS had other plans. The CCP and Mr. Wang of MSS were preparing for Jian Wu to move smoothly into the next phase of his adult life in service of country and use Jian to enter the Taiwan island as a low-level spy. Their new plan was to be executed in a very weird sort of way without triggering the Western powers and the MOSSAD noticing the "bait and switch" technique that the Chinese used when they want to move someone across the water into Taiwan.

The fight sequence was right before the eyes of his handlers and with little information flowing to the MSS and other alliances who would be made aware latter in the week. The MSS believed there were leaks in every Triad organization and that it would be difficult to plug all leaks.

The Big Fight

Jian Wu weaved to the left, then feigned to the right and then took off airborne.

He left the ground and used the two-foot double kick that landed on Mr. K's head directly from the front with Jian's left leg hit the bald head and deflected to hit K's right shoulder breaking it with a loud crack and Jian's right leg slid off the bald head glancing towards the left shoulder blade and with the brute force of impact dislocated the left arm from the left shoulder. The pain was excruciating and there was a silent moan that echoed through the night stadium.

The double foot kick strike was fatal and knocked out K.

Mr. K was pole-axed and went backwards and hit the floor with a resounding thud. Mr. K was out cold. This was unexpected and even the WOP TU who were at the fight were so startled by the fight sequence that they did not have time to respond to the double kick and almost instantaneous thud. Ten seconds and their K champion was out for the count. Jian was officially the winner, unless it could be proven that he had cheated.

The crowd was on their feet and the uproar was heard in the next province.

The fight was over before it started. People paid to see long and entertaining fights. Nobody came to see a 30 second fight or less. It was over before it started.

They also gambled good money and it would be a pity if the underdog won in a few seconds.

"What was the possibility that this could happen with the odds in favor of Mr. K winning?"

"Was the Fight fixed?" there were loud murmurs in the crowd.

The rumbles in the crowd were growing and this usually did not end well.

Jian stood over the still fighter and realized that K was "out for the count." NO movement from the prostate fighter.

He said to himself: "Should I kill him or should I let him live."

"Kill him!! Kill K!!," shouts from the screaming crowd.

Expletive from Jian's lips as he scanned the

angry crowd. The crowd might kill him as he leaves the octagon.

Jian kicked K in the chest cavity with a massive kick to the rib cage area.

"K is dead!! Should I kill him again??" Jian muttered under his breath.

K appeared to have passed into the next world. K was in a coma or dead.

Jian bent over and tested for a pulse. There was none.

Jian Wu, walked out of the octagon, a "free man" and exited the MMA and cage fighting arena for good. There was no going back for him. That is what Jian thought.

Little did he know what was waiting for him if he survived the next few hours. The WOP TU chiefs were still trying to figure out what happened. Some did not even know how much money was lost by the big WOP TU guys.

Once the guys figured out the extent of the losses, they would be shouting for blood and Jian would be dead, his family would be chopped to little bits and fed to the pigs owned by them. Jian was running from the area.

Some of his friends warned him to keep a large distance from Canton, possibly escape to the north of China. Jian had no plan of action, and he was not able to think on his feet. He had to contact the MSS soon or else he will get smoked by the WOP TU.

He knew that this was very bad for his family, but he could not do anything about it. He was concerned about his mom, but his dad was supposed to handle the family business by himself.

Susie Wong

Jian Wu's sister, Susie was born three years after him. Although Susie was younger to Jian, she was maturing fast. This was typical of most Chinese girls who matured between 8 and 12 years of age. Susie hit puberty before her 10th birthday.

Susie was able to grasp the meaning of life and matured before Jian. Jian hit puberty at about 12 years of age but was still growing physically in his teen years. Mentally maturity was slow for the boys and the women matured quickly in China.

Susie was moved to a cousin's home at the age of two. They had no kids of their own, so they adopted Susie as their own child. Susie was conscientious and hard working. She kept her grades high and helped around the Wong household. She was a welcome addition in the Wong family.

Susie Wong loved western cowboy stories

and viewed herself as a local Chinese version of an "American Cowboy." The 'Cowboy' term was foreign to China and many of her friends did not get it. No matter, she continued to live in her head and even developed a very manly walk as she moved in the school yard and the local playgrounds. The kids made fun of her strange behavior.

She playacted "Cowboys and Indians" and was always heard whistling tunes from some well-known Western cowboy films. Her classmates thought she was strange and tried to avoid her. She would be chasing phantom ghosts around the school playground. Her friends assumed that this behavior would disappear as she grew older. Nothing changed and Susie was still the tomboy as she reached her teen years.

"She is too much trouble, Talks about tomboys and dresses like a Cowboy." "This child is trouble," gossiped the middle-aged ladies in the village.

"I am excited to know that the others think I am strange!" Susie muttered under her breath.

"There are lots of crazies around the school." Her friend Mai said.

"Susie and I are a fringe group and once they get it, they will accept us as we are." Mai continued.

Mai was a more balanced individual, and she

liked Susie and was ready to stay friends with her for the foreseeable future.

Susie kept to herself and although quite pretty, she tried not to attract attention. She avoided the various groups at school. There was the Nerds, the "A-Team" and the "Crackpots". She avoided The "A-Team." And tolerated the other two groups.

She had one good friend - "Mai." Mai stayed out of trouble, Susie and Mai stuck together. They got along fine and avoided any skirmishes with the "Nerds", "The A-team" or "the Crackpots."

The "Nerds" were the ones who studied and were oblivious of anything but their books, education, and the library. They did not participate in physical activities and sports or get into gossip or mess with the opposite sex.

The Nerds were very single minded in getting into the top college for their college education. Sex was not discussed and considered taboo in that group. Susie and Mai's success pact with their parents was quite like the Nerds, and they did not care about makeup or clothes or beautification.

Susie and Mai played with their mobile devices, tablets, and cell phones but did not notice or interfere with boys or other girls. The Nerds were male dominated. The women nerds imitated the boy or male nerds.

Women nerds wanted to be the best and even dreamed of beating the male nerds. Expectations ran high among the female nerds. This one "up-women-ship" was going to get these women into weird situations. This was not going to end well.

The A-Team was a bunch of losers, who thought about themselves as "the winners." They had a very high opinion about their looks, brains, and everything in between. They would do anything to look good and perfect. They even purchased top-of-the-line designer brands and rarely used these clothing more than once in a month. In fact, they would use these clothing once or twice before throwing them away. The A-team were not smart with money, and they believed in spending money on street collectibles, paintings, drawings, and useless hand-me-downs. They hung with the same group and did not venture far from their tribe.

The A-Team was headed for serious monetary trouble and would eventually live under a bridge or by a stream. Food was trivial for them and they could survive with one or two pieces of fried won ton.

The "crackpots" were a group of mental cases. They took risks and were likely to get caught as they crossed the line into minor crimes making it difficult to rein them in. They were designated by the "crackpot" term. They did not believe in limits and they went all in. Some indulged in gambling, prostitution and sniffed everything they could get their hands on. This group would land in some rehab camp and would be sent North to the labor camps in Daqing. Or the Northern border camps for rehabilitation.

There were other groups within the school and many groups were fragmented and just comprised a few persons and hence they did not get traction in the school. There was the "Party animals", "Shop till you drop" and "Junk eaters."

Some of these groups existed in the outgroups or away from the school premises. Jian was considered a member of the outgroup that was involved in dangerous combat situations and street-fighting. Jian was a loner and he did not believe in having a fan base. He received adulation from some of the male and female classmates, but he would let anyone convince him about creating a group for the underground fight circle.

Susie was considered by her advisors as "most likely to succeed" and that got her into the American equivalent of "Gifted and Talented." She was learning languages at a remarkable rate. She mastered some of the Romanic languages in her first two years of secondary school. She started to learn other languages like English, Gaelic, and the European languages. She was moved into a "Special" Class, and this was to prepare her for challenging careers like the foreign service and spy craft. She was sent for advanced training in Guns, hand-to hand combat and all sorts of tricks of the spy trade.

The "Special" class of warriors were selected by Chinese trainers for advanced learning. Teenagers and young adults who fell into this group would be "the trained professionals of tomorrow." The success rate was not expected to be very high, but even at 50 percent, that was meant to bring China into the twenty first century.

Susie was going to be top in her class of trained fighters, assassins. She was sent to Sniper school. Her calm nerves and ability to work under pressure, put her in a special class. Her pinpoint accuracy and marksmanship to hit a small coin or token at one thousand feet, put her in a special class: "Above the rest."

China needs more clones like 'Susie'. They were looking far and wide to get a class of professional fighters like Susie. As time passes by, with the middle class growing, the attraction to fight or be part of the special forces was not attractive to the Chinese youth or young adults. They preferred easy lifestyles and were not willing to lose their blood on the battlefield. The days of the "give your life for the Motherland" were slowly receding into the past memory. It was interesting to believe in this concept in the abstract, but it was quite devastating to do it in reality.

The Millennials wanted to make money and travel abroad to study and work in the United States or Europe. China did not offer the wealth accumulation that the West offered. You worked hard and you made it to the top in the West. The freedom that you won was more than just the money. Power and ownership of private property and luxuries like condos, boats, planes. Freedom to travel and to have free expression and ability to make money and run the enterprise were all attractive options. A concept that was remote to the CCP.

They understood the need for self-expression in China, but if the Chinese people were allowed that freedom, it would lead to Chaos. Chinese Party officials were afraid of the one billion population having the freedom to choose their own party officials, so elections were out. Those poisonous ideas belonged to the West and was fine for the democratic and chaotic ruling in most western countries. India, their neighbor was an example of

Chaos with a billion people in the voting pool and that was an example that China did not want to mimic.

China was very protective of their laws (if any) and were not interested in changing the laws to make it easy to own land, businesses, and other essential products. Chinese youth were looking for improvement in their living standards and style.

Chinese people are starting to travel abroad, and while visiting abroad, they are noticing how people live all over the world, even in Third World countries. So "Why is China holding its people back?"

Susie Wong's mental faculties were superb, and she was cognizant of the danger of her position. When in combat she had experienced the eyes of the enemy and could kill without any thought or hesitation. Her last kill on the Indian border was almost reflexive, no thought was involved. She went into the kill mode and hit the other soldier between the eyes. The bullet killed the enemy combatant and she saw the life go out of the soldier.

One moment there was movement, next there was none. The enemy soldier or combatant just fell in one swift slow motion and was dead before he hit the ground. She combed the area to check the dead combatant and the vicinity and see if there was anyone coming but did not see any other enemy soldiers within 100 feet of the dead soldier. She quickly exited the place before she became a target of a sniper on the surrounding hills.

When Susie got back to base to debrief the sortie and the kill, the commander was surprised that there was only one soldier loitering in that part of the enemy territory. Much of this area was not clearly demarcated as Indian or Chinese zones. The Line of Control was running along the banks of the large cold stream and there were many spots on either side that were disputed by both countries.

WOP TU STREET JUSTICE

The Wop Tu thugs were waiting for Jian. Their bosses had lost tons of money on this fight. Their beatings would be severe and debilitating. They pounded him from all sides. When he fell to the ground, they kicked him on all sides. Kicks to his abdomen, kidneys, and chest. Some of the hits were glancing ones, others directed to his internal organs. This was a man who had taken heavy hits to his body. He was no stranger to beatings – both in the ring and on the street.

He knew through the pain of the beatings that he would go unconscious. He was transitioning between conscious and un-conscious and willing that the beatings would stop. The triads were good at delivering this systematic punishment and could pulverize his internal organs and make his muscles into mush.

"I hope this beating will end soon." Jian was mumbling in pain.

Pottery Making

"Throw the worthless piece of dirt." The Wop Tu commander spat out in guttural street Cantonese.

Four thugs grabbed the badly injured man, beaten mercilessly and threw him from the overpass to his death.

"Do not come back from the dead." Blurted the leader, "If you are seen again, you will be sliced with a meat cleaver."

The Triads are very brutal. The meat cleaver is their implement of torture and slow painful death. The Wop Tu was known for their version of a thousand cuts, where they sliced pieces of meat from a person, thin slices. They kept the person alive through the pain and the slicing. This primitive form of killing was known as "Lingchi", translated variously as the slow process, the lingering death of slow slicing also known as death by a thousand cuts. It was a form of torture and execution used in China from nine hundred until 1905. It was also used in Vietnam and Korea. Better known as "Disambiguation" This is meant to torture persons using psychological cutting methods. It is believed that if you keep this going, a professional killer could kill you over several days. This beats a bullet through the brain. The person would be begging you as their nerves were screaming: "Just kill me and do it quickly."

Jian needed more than luck to survive this vertical drop of 20 feet to the road below the overpass. He went over the side and hit the moving truck bed filled with rotting produce for the restaurant market in Shenzhen. The landing jarred his body and blood started to ooze out of his many wounds. He groaned and fell into a troubled sleep. The bouncing woke him up as he went from intermittent sleep to partially awake with pain and agony from his many torn muscles and cracked ribs. However, he was no stranger to wounds, rib abrasions and worse and his body had learned to heal itself. He needed plenty of bed rest and Chinese medicine to heal his wounds. Food, medicine, and water for his dehydrated body. Some of the Chinese meds would do wonders to the broken body.

Jian was hit by the headlights as the truck navigated around bends. This continuous motion, poor quality truck shocks and headlights kept him partially awake. As the early light of dawn creeped into the Eastern sky, he realized he was approaching the outskirts of Shenzhen. They were headed East and South to hit the port city of Shenzhen. Shenzhen had grown from the small export zone to the granite and steel city about six times the size of Hong Kong. A City that barely housed expatriates of a million plus in the nineties was now bustling with about ten million plus.

Shenzhen City was very prosperous and had many street gangs and police who kept the peace and where necessary applied plenty of pressure on the local populace. Its proximity to Hong Kong and its zoning statutes made the City quite aggressive in world trade. The CCP wanted a large amount of its manufacturing and new production to be completed within ten miles of the city. The pollution was getting worse.

By five in the morning, the truck was on the outskirts of Shenzhen City. The sounds changed, and the truck was bouncing on city grade asphalt. Jian woke up in pain. He was wide awake. Need to jump from the truck before it gets to its destination.

Two days of combats in the octagon and lack of sleep had exhausted the fighter. The final beating from the Wop Tu was over the top. As the truck slowed down, Jian slid from the truck followed by a painful roll-on uneven surface. He did not feel any more pain. He came to in a few minutes, felt like he was asleep for an hour on the side of the road.

"I need to find a safe house in Shenzhen and cross into Hong Kong." Jian needed to get out of mainland China and quick.

Jian was mumbling to himself. He needed a mobile and contact to Mr. Wang of the MSS.

"Disguise, passport, visas and papers – Money and contacts." Jian's mind was in turmoil. "Max 3 to 4 days in Hong Kong or Macau" "If the Wop Tu find me, I will not be worth a tiny Chinese pebble…"

Mr. Wang Xia & the MSS

Mr. Wang Xia was a senior officer of the MSS, The civilian security, intelligence, and secret police agency of the People's Republic of China, responsible for counterintelligence within China, foreign intelligence, and political security. Its military counterpart is the Intelligence Bureau of the Joint Staff. It is headquartered in Beijing with subordinate branches at the provincial, city, municipality, and township levels throughout China. It is one of the most secretive intelligence organizations in the world.

Mr. Wang Xia controls a vast network of operatives in the South China Sea, Hainan Island, Hong Kong Territory, and Taiwan. The logo of the MSS is unique among Chinese government agencies. It displays the emblem of the Chinese Communist Party.

Mr. Wang had served under previous intelligence

chiefs and had achieved his title of Senior "Pottery Maker" from his various efforts that had managed to overthrow and control various situations in China, post-earthquakes, dam collapses, and the various situations that could have resulted in instability like Tiananmen Square in 1989.

Tiananmen gets its name from "Gate of Heavenly Peace" first constructed in 1417. It covers 100 acres (40.5 hectares) and each flagstone is numbered for ease in assembly of Parades. Once it was the Main gate to the Forbidden City. June 4, 1989 was a tough day and the unrest was put down by the Communist Party. What started in April 1989, ended by a brutal repressive attack on the student revolution.

In an autocratic state, nothing was left to chance.

Wang's main role was to have a finger on the pulse of the youth and the other maturing 20s male and female population who could trigger riots on school and college campuses. He had spies on all campuses, union halls, and worker places. He worked to regulate the frustration and keep it at a manageable level. Youth are frustrated worldwide. But one had to learn to divert their frustrations by letting them vent via distractions: sports, underground activities like cage fighting, as long as it was not directed at the communist party.

It looked like a very simple effort, but it was complicated by the internet, the smart phone market and now the mobility of the Chinese population, especially the youth of the 21st Century.

Premier Xi's directive was to keep everything within direct control of the Lenin-Maoist doctrine. If there was any liberalization of the societal thinking, China would explode into civil war. Keep the people fed, happy and growing rich.

Mr. Wang's grades for these direct reports were from 'A' to 'F.' Jian was a definite 'A+' and he had very great potential for development as an asset and would be used for overseas contracts and sleeper cell efforts.

Mr. Wang was keeping Jian at arms-length but monitoring his every move. He needed continuous feedback from his spies and personnel who were not aware of the number of opportunities they had to destroy Jian's career inadvertently. However, the less they knew the better. It was always on a need-to-know basis.

Wang Xia did not spend much time sending reports to the provincial heads or the Beijing Chiefs. He would go up to Beijing when he was called and keep his bosses abreast of what was going on in the south China Sea. He did not have to send budget requests or constant reminders. Money would come to him, and his staff would be provided with the money they needed to stay operational. Bureaucracy was the death sentence of many a good top-secret organization, but unlimited funds were not to be misspent.

Wang Xia was aware of his responsibilities, and he kept his organization very nimble with the funds that were provided. He kept tabs on personal expenses and expenses of his teams, but he did not want the operation to collapse because of a lack of funds.

Helen's Search and Exit to Hong Kong

Helen Tsai got the news a day later that something terrible had happened to Jian. The news was sketchy and incomplete and came to her in bits and scrambled pieces that she pieced together to make sense of what happened to Jian. She was beside herself as she could not locate him around town and wondered what had happened to Jian. She went to all the usual places and talked to all the usual suspects. There was no information. That was not good. She talked to her mum and was unable to get support to widen her search. Her mother indicated that he would appear just as he had disappeared. Helen knew that this was not true and, in her heart, she felt that he was needing her to show up at his side.

The next day, she talked to some 'wise guys.' These 'wise guys' were on the fringes of their student bodies but were not part of any criminal enterprise. Some were aspiring small time crooks and thieves. None of them had a clue. This was really getting weird. She had to get information to Jian's parents who seemed to be concerned but were not surprised that he did not show up the previous two evenings. Rumors were going through the rumor mill that Jian had a falling out with his caretakers and was being hunted.

Helen got a clear message from a good friend that Jian had left town in a hurry and was beaten by the Wop Tu thugs. There was no precise understanding of what really happened and why Jian had disappeared off the face of the earth and that his folks did not know where he had gone. She finally got a hint that he was possibly headed to Shenzhen and eventually to the Hong Kong Special Administrative Region.

She decided to travel light and head to Hong Kong in the early evening. Time was of the essence and she did not want to lose the one important person in her life.

Helen Tsai arrived in Shenzhen and took the ferry to Hong Kong and was scouring the streets of the Wan Chai Metropolitan area situated at the western part of the Wan Chai District on the northern shore of Hong Kong Island. It is Hong

Kong's red-light zone. The Triads have their fingers everywhere and especially in the red-light zone, and they watch everyone who enters and leaves the area. They do not like strangers wandering around asking questions.

"That is bad for business" they murmur to their close friends.

"Who is this woman and what does she want with this character she is searching for? She must be looking for her lover?"

"This is never good for business when a somewhat pretty lady is wandering in the Wan Chai area asking questions about a Friend?"

People were getting restless and the information was going back to the Heads in their lairs. The directive that came down was

"Get rid of this damsel and do it asap" The Triad Chief instructed.

They sent two scrawny and mean shadows to follow Helen. She was not aware of her shadows. She was making inquiries about Jian's whereabouts in her mother tongue and the queries were trickling back to the Triad Chiefs. The Triads wanted to ensnare Jian, but they were not sure if he could be tricked into walking into a trap in Hong Kong.

Meanwhile, Jian was getting feedback from his contacts in the Wan Chai area that a pretty lady was making inquiries about him. Looked like Helen Tsai had made it to Hong Kong. If she could track him down in less than a week, the bad guys would be very close behind. Not good for him staying underground.

He headed into the Wan Chai area, but with a minor disguise to make him look slightly older. He was worried that Helen was attracting undue attention while he was trying to recover from his multiple injuries and broken ribs. This was complicating his recovery and escape plans.

He was worried sick and was staring into the mirror, while inspecting his disguise.

"Who am I?" he queries.

"What is happening to me?" he mumbles, "Am I performing the right move?" Jian says.

"Am I walking into a dangerous area with no backup?" Jian says.

"I have my fists, broken body and might not be able to defend myself. I am walking into a trap set by Helen's weaknesses and the Wop Tu Triad; they are merely using Helen as bait." Jian continues.

"What are my options?? Do I have any options or alternatives?" Jian asks.

"When you care for someone, you have to take

risks or else..." He embraces the danger that he was facing.

He gets to the Wan Chai area where Helen was last seen. The street appears very busy and there is trouble on all sides.

"Somebody could put a knife in my back." Jian says.

He is very circumspect and walks in wider and wider circles, but his gait and movement are slow and painful. Which is what he wants and needs at this critical juncture of his life.

He sees Helen and she looks tired and irascible. Not a good situation.

At this time, she would likely make a bad decision and would be unable to follow directives from Jian.

She is sipping a cup of green tea and looking hungry and badly in need of nutrition.

"What is happening to her. She has aged within a week or less." He mumbles.

"This Helen woman needs to get with the program and look the part of a civilian spy." Says Jian to himself.

He passes by her table without a sideways glance, and he picks up the shadows, one on the north side of the square and another on the south side.

"Something is not right here." Jian ponders.

He had to assume that these guys have mobile phones and links with their heads or supervisors. A wrong move and he would have the whole gang in the area. He would be dragged away and killed or maybe given a slow death.

The options were not many for Jian and Helen.

There would be more characters in the vicinity watching Helen and appearing disinterested. He could not be sure, but he had to move quickly.

He slips behind the north shadow. He drags him into the darkness and applies pressure on his neck and knocks him out. Another quick blow to the head and the shadow is silent and is done with. The shadow does not make a sound. Just a slight moan as he goes down.

Jian pulls the north shadow further into the darkness and places him in a partially sitting position against a wall. This is good and he needs to proceed to the south shadow.

"One down, second to go. So far, so good!!" Jian mumbles.

He then takes a wider arc to get behind the south shadow. He hurries to get behind the other guy and then realizes the south shadow has moved from his location. Time has passed and the situation has changed. This is a dynamic situation and Jian needs to proceed with caution.

Pottery Making

He turns around just in time as the second shadow brings the hard wooden object onto his head. The blow would have been fatal if it had made direct contact to his head. His instinct and quick response allows him the milliseconds to get out of the way. If not, Helen and he would have been dead in a matter of minutes.

The sudden movement in his peripheral vision; Jian pivots and diverts the blow directed at his head away from his vulnerable head and body parts.

The object deflects and hits a glancing blow to his arm. The pain shoots up his arm to his shoulder and he winces with pain. He had enough of injuries to last him a lifetime and this one is worse than the previous blows he had received to the arm.

It hurts like hell, and he goes down on his knees. He is cursing under his breath and trying to clear the stars floating around. His head clears, his vision returns and he is coming back to the land of the living.

He instinctively grabs the hands of the attacker and buries his leg into the groin while applying pressure on the attacker's voice box. The attacker drops like a sack of potatoes. The guy releases a guttural sound coming from deep in his throat. Jian looks around to see if anyone is paying attention to him. No one notices this altercation with the shadow. The shadow was dead before he hit the ground.

"I need to get out of here." Jian mutters in pain.

He turns around to see if Helen is still in the same position.

Their eyes met and she realizes that the danger is passed. He signals for her to move to the west. He circles and comes quickly to her side. They need to get out of Wan Chai area and back to the Kowloon side and the safety of the small hotel that Jian resides in.

Helen is amazed at the speed at which Jian reacts and feels that she made the right decision to come to him. She will have to stay by his side. Although injured from the numerous fights and recent Wop Tu beating, the confrontation with the two shadows, Jian was recovering quickly.

He needs some care and healing cream applied to his various wounds. He feels good with Helen's proximity and her love for him. He needs tender loving care (TLC) and somebody to watch his back.

This is how they will have to proceed on their next leg of their journey. Jian will have to inform Wang that he will have to move two persons on the next leg of their journey. Paperwork will be required for Helen Tsai too. While they lay low for a few days, eating good soup and light food, Jian was getting strong and improving in his recovery and strength.

On the other hand, his lover Helen was also getting quite calm and feeling that the two of them would be quite an unbeatable team. Love and teamwork were going to help them develop in the weeks, months ahead. Helen sent a coded message to her mom that all is well and they were healing ever so slowly.

Helen did not have any ideas about their affection for each other. She did not want to get in the way and be an unnecessary burden to Jian. At the same time, she was hoping she could assist Jian in his pursuit to be a useful MSS operative

Change of Travel Plans

Mr. Wang was not excited about this sudden change of plans, but he will have to work his magic.

Wang gets Jian and Helen across to Macau, which was a Portuguese territory, and now controlled by the Mainland Chinese as a Special Administrative Region. The HK -Zhuhai-Macau bridge is a 34-mile bridge with three spans across the Pearl River Delta. Jian and Helen make it to Macau via the long bridge.

Wang now creates a whole new profile for Jian Wu and Helen Tsai. They change his name and build a profile that will completely alter his image before he appears on foreign soil. Jian is changed to "John." The back stopping, and build-up of his fake record: schools, family life, and other information completely change him to a clean and wholesome image. There will be no mention of cage fighting and combats in the underground.

Wang needs to produce a completely new person. Helen will stay the same and use her name to continue her travels and exploits in a foreign country.

Jian Wu aka John Wu is now portrayed as a person who grew up in Chengdu, China. His school, his extra-curricular stuff, his background has changed to a sweet, soft-spoken, bilingual Mandarin and English-speaking person with an acquired American accent. He will need more time and practice to sound real. The Taiwan Secret Service and the CIA will not be fooled, and he needs to be on his A game. Helen will have to pass as his fiancée and eventually his wife.

John (Jian) Wu is not yet ready for primetime. Helen was another challenge and Wang was ready to give her more time to adjust to her role as John's fiancée.

Their papers needed to be able to pass inspection anywhere in the world.

Susie on the Move

Meanwhile, Susie Wong was also preparing for her transition to the West. She was unaware of her brothers' situation in southern China, Macau, Hong Kong, and Taiwan.

Wang or Jian's handler was in a different hierarchy of the intelligence wing. Susie was in a very tough para-military unit: (Delta forces equivalent) and although there was no romantic special forces moniker like "Seal Team Six," she was given a class or Tier. Equivalent.

There are 7000 to 14000 special operations troops. They are known as rapid-response soldiers in the event of limited regional war and used under high-tech conditions. They carry out commando, counterterrorism, and intelligence gathering operations.

Many of these forces were used in escalation fights with Indian forces in Lehi, Tibet. This is a part of Northeast Kashmir and considered disputed territory as the British had not drawn a clear line between India, Pakistan, and Tibet. China has occupied Tibet and this area is now considered an extension of the Chinese autonomous zones.

China has plans to build roads across the mountains and valleys of Northern Pakistan and parts of Tibet and Occupied Kashmir. They have already built a road across permafrost Tibet and even a railroad from Beijing to Lhasa in Tibet. China is making many incursions into Indian territory and recently have extended their special forces into India and other countries that are a potential threat to China.

In the last conflict with Vietnam, the Vietnamese special forces caused substantial trouble and destroyed the morale of the Chinese forces in 1979 and 1980. China was embarrassed by those attacks. The Vietnamese forces were trained via their 25 years of combat with the French and American forces. They were battle-tested and ready.

Lessons learnt from the Vietnam war have been applied in their 23 December 2008 encounter with the Somali pirates in the Arabian sea to protect the Chinese commercial ships.

The Special forces are used all over the place. Susie Wong has learned the hard lessons in various combat situations and was promoted to a senior officer and moved to higher operations on the Indian border against land forces.

Susie would be very useful and will be utilized because of her language skills in Taiwan, Europe, and United States.

There is much to be taught to their special operational forces and China is expanding to have between 30,000 and 60,000 operational troops worldwide. Many will be on their ships, submarines, and their newly made islands. **Many of the Chinese mainland troops are trained for an invasion of Taiwan. China's policy is leaning on making Taiwan a part of China by 2030.**

China's policy is to occupy Taiwan without firing a bullet. It has considered Taiwan to be a part of China mainland. The re-unification of Taiwan China was a doctrine of the CCP and they were willing to go to lengths to make Taiwan a part of China. China has patience on how they would go about it. They believe it was an internal situation and needed to be resolved by the Chinese people: Republic of China (ROC) and Mainland China (PRC). Other countries like the United States and Europe should not interfere. They do not want to get into a major conflict with Taiwan like the Russians have done in Ukraine.

Pottery Making

Susie did not have a controller for the first 10 years as she developed her combat and analytical skills. Eventually, they appointed a very competent and professional manager: Mr. Xi Wen, who is now in his forties and was an ex-special forces soldier who had run major operations in Iran, Iraq, and Northern Europe. He had short stints in the US. The quick stints are run in East Coast cities and were 3-to-5-day operations.

Mr. Xi was a strategist and he believed in keeping the Americans on their toes. Quick on his feet and constant improvisation gave Xi an advantage against the Americans and Europeans. He spoke many languages without an accent. He had studied in Europe and had been trained in colloquialisms, idiosyncrasies, and mannerisms of the American and European spies. His team had penetrated different organizations: EU, USAID, Peace Corps, and the United Nations Peace Council.

Susie would need to be pulled from the operational force into the cloak and dagger stuff and would need specialized training to running strategic operations in Taiwan, Europe and eventually the United States. The Sleeper cells (SSATs) would need to be activated in the next two to three years. If not, they should be active by the 2030s.

SSATs was starting to be awakened in Asia and

their reach and impact would need to be moved to Europe and simultaneously setup a cell in Hawaii and Alaska. The United States has many active forces monitoring all channels, but their focus is terrorism (Domestic and Middle Eastern). They have other cells that are monitoring the African and Asian Terrorist groups.

Susie would need to be able to travel between the two American Western most states and start observing the United States preparations in retaliation for a China attack on Taiwan. United States was underestimating that the Chinese would not attempt an attack at this time. That is not a great assumption to make.

"He will win who knows when to fight and when not to fight." Sun Tzu

China was thinking otherwise. We have Hong Kong in the bag and we need to move on to the other properties like Taiwanese islands and other disputed islands in the South China sea. Some islands are far away from Taiwan and will be difficult to protect.

Taiwan Present Day

Taiwan is across from China at one hundred miles across the Taiwan Straits. The closest City to Taiwan on the mainland is Xiamen which is about five miles across the water from Kinmen County Island. Kinmen belongs to Taiwan and they have a fighting force on the island for quick response.

China can devastate the Kinmen County island of 130,000 inhabitants. Taiwan island and Taipei is about one hundred miles from Donhaiwan in the north and 110 miles from Xiamen on the coast.

Attack on Taiwan seemed imminent in early 2021. China is running sorties of 30 to 50 attack aircraft into the contested waters south of Taiwan. Some of the aircraft are cutting the southern corner of the Taiwan airspace. The new President of Taiwan, Tsai Ing-wen is a smooth-talking politician. Her credentials are phenomenal and being a woman, she is considered the best candidate for China to start their romance with Taiwan. She talks tough, but when the time comes, she will not bring Taiwan into a direct conflict with mainland Chinese people. She believes that this will not end well. She is pragmatic and would like the two Chinas to work out a clean unification program. She knows what happened in Hong Kong and is not under any illusion that the Chinese in Beijing will follow a gentle course with Taiwan.

China is starting to make overtures towards Taiwan based on their 30-year history with Hong Kong. They are talking about "one country, two systems." China has used the same language before in Hong Kong, but their dealing with their own Chinese people: Nationalists from the Kuomintang who have settled in Taiwan (formerly known as Formosa) and hopefully the bad blood and the past is buried over the 70 years of peace and quiet over the Taiwan Straits.

Thoughts across Taiwan or the Republic of China (ROC) are summarized below:

"Should Taiwan declare a war?"

"Can they declare a war? China is a behemoth. It is political suicide."

"Why is China goading Taiwan into a war?"

"But what will come of it?" "Americans are sleepwalking over their own problems and may not come to Taiwan's assistance until it is too late."

The Americans are logistically too far away to participate in a war with China. Even a controlled assault to protect Taiwan would be too much for the American people to even ponder. After two failed skirmishes in Iraq and Afghanistan, the American people are very skittish about these wars across the Atlantic and the Pacific.

The Chinese can invade Taiwan and take the island in a matter of days or weeks. Taiwan could put up resistance, but China has amassed Sea power, land forces and air forces.

There are a million Chinese soldiers ready to go to war to occupy Taiwan. The fighting will be intense and involve hand-to-hand combat and urban street fighting, and China is not going to give it a second thought.

Taiwan cannot win this war. Even if it opposes the invasion, there will be destruction of several cities, towns, and manufacturing plants. The Supply chain will be disrupted, that inflation worldwide will go sky high in the years ahead.

More than a million Taiwanese persons will be killed. A larger number of Chinese people will be killed.

War is ugly and there will be losers on both sides.

Pottery Making – Taiwanese Style

*J*ohn aka Jian Wu, Ministry of State Security (MSS) employee, was a shadow Guo Anbu (Guojia Anquan Bu) operative. The Ministry of State Security or Guojia Anquan bu, is the civilian intelligence, security, and secret police agency of the People's Republic of China, responsible for counterintelligence, foreign intelligence, and political security.

Luo Da Wei was head of the MSS, and he was tough and kept a low profile in People's Republic of China reporting directly to the Chinese Premier. No TV interviews or radio chats. No public image or answering questions on National TV. There were dark hidden accounts with funds that were not managed by the Finance Ministry or the Treasury.

This Number 2 Account was managed by the Premier's office and used for State Security and there was no overseer or General Accounting Office apportioning funds or money for State Security. If more money was needed, more money would be apportioned or allocated. State Security was a very opaque organization with minimum State or Federal Controls. The Military was a separate organization with plenty of Federal controls at all levels. To manage security in the Country, the Premier knew that money for the special forces and China's protection and security, there would have to be enough funding to keep the lights on at night.

There was no oversight of this part of the Federal Economy. Mr. Wang was given massive power over the funding. With that power, there was responsibility. If Mr. Wang mismanaged the funds, that would be damaging to him and his family. Mr. Xi, the Premier believed that this funding had very tough accountability and could end in disaster, if there was any inkling that Mr. Wang had his hands in the Jar, Mr. Wang would disappear and not be found again.

Jian Wu receives a call from his hidden-from-sight handler: six-fingered Wang. Wang is ruthless in his dealings with his direct reports. He keeps his team in a tightly controlled circle: "only need-to-know" basis. Jian Wu will be sent to the promised land via Macau, Taiwan, Vancouver, and California. There was various levels of testing and degrees of responsibility. Every level would come with more risks and more chances of errors and losing his life.

The Project in Taiwan would be of limited duration and would last a brief period. It was a test phase for the team. The environment was to test Jian and his team in a fast-moving project with limited expectations and quick results. The Taiwan forces were always in a state of alert. This project was to test how ready the enemy was. Taiwanese armed forces were a very small percentage of the population (about 1%). The other 99% were not in a state of readiness. However, there were small teams of militia leaders who believed that they need to train to prepare for an all-out war.

The Taiwan militia was a loose amalgamation of persons mostly ex-military and para-military young men and some women who had spent a couple of years in military school. However, these twenty-year-old had tended to forget their training and were unable to recall what was taught to them several years in their late teens.

The militia were starting their own local training and given support from special rangers and equipment supplied by the military. As the time was to utilize the weekends and holiday periods, the time was not sufficient to provide these low-level fighters any opportunity to be prepared for an attack from the mainland.

Jian was a good and trained person and had spent a lot of time preparing for this attack and his effort to get into the military wing.

The questions in Jian's mind "Was anyone in the West really monitoring him? Did they even know that he existed?"

Wang believed that "The CIA, MI5 and MI6, KGB, FSB … were all watching the secret service in China." "That means him and his local and remote bosses in Beijing."

What about the various people under him or the unknowns who were coming out of school and were generally not considered like professional guys.

He always intoned in his Hunan dialect:" Do not underestimate the Big Boys in Taiwan or America?"

"One could never be sure, even the Mossad, Middle East teams, Iranians, and others were keeping tabs on China's secret service."

Wang was paranoid by nature and suspicious of everyone including the triads who operated in the south of China and the various Chinatowns in big cities. The Triads like the Tongs were opportunistic and took advantage of anyone as long as there was money in it. They did not owe allegiance to any country or rule of law. They would "jump ship" depending on the amount of money that was involved. The Americans and the Western Nations knew about that and were continuously forcing money into the Triads and Tongs.

Leaks were many and although there were major efforts to clean up the remote sites, one could never be sure.

Wang had never been to the United States. The Americans were watching his every move and had a dossier about two inches thick. Every operative or person he met and followed; every person after their meetings to establish several degrees of control. Nothing should be left to chance. The message to Jian Wu would have to be delivered via subterfuge and dropped on his person, coat, jacket pocket. No eye contact, no signaling or even speaking directly to him. Jian and a bunch of agents were the unknown factors and Wang wanted to keep these guys in the dark hidden column.

The United States had just left Afghanistan and the American people were tired of war and occupation.

"How would the Americans counter the Taiwan attack?" Question in everyone's minds.

Susie and her team of special forces were activated to assist Jian and Helen in their Taiwan landing plan. The complicated maneuver at sea and landing on the Northeast coast of Taiwan would require special assistance from this team and needed some smuggler gangs to aid in creating distraction at sea on the Southwest and close to the Taiwanese islands. If the Taiwanese Coast Guards were kept off balance, there would be plenty of time for the landing team (small) to get to the East Coast and land near the Longdong Bay Promontory.

Susie led her team and created all sorts of diversions on the Xiamen Coast. Little did she realize that the landing craft was bearing her brother and future sister-in-law on an essential mission into Taiwan.

Taiwan Landing Plan

"There were eyes and ears everywhere. Electronic devices and even their breathing was monitored by these Taiwanese devils."

Some Chinese Politburo guys were under the impression that the Russians were the good guys and need to be trusted within limits. Wang did not trust the Russians one little bit. In the Intelligence units, trust was hard to come by and the rule of the road:

"Trust no one and no one trusts you." Wang lived by this saying.

He named the operation to penetrate his young team into Taiwan as "ONE HUNG LOW" It was a subtle joke with no significance and did not connote any meaning, so the Americans, Taiwanese, MOSSAD, and other spies could spend their whole lives trying to figure this one.

"ONE HUNG LOW" was not a major cost operation, but it would need to be effective and with short, medium, and long-range objectives. In the short term, there would need to be at least 8 to 10 medium spies or analysts: 60 percent men and 40 percent women. Rather than move them as teams, we will move them in all sorts of fractals: a one-person team, two-person team and even a three-person team.

As Wang started to organize John and Helen's move to Taiwan. The waters across the Taiwan Strait were actively monitored both by the Chinese and Taiwanese speed boats and submarines. It was not a place for the weak of heart, so the transportation had to be done in the dead of night or via an airdrop. It was not pleasant for his people to have a welcoming committee as they came down from the sky.

Analysis of this airdrop method was not approved and they decided to use a low noise, average speed small hovercraft that would leave from Fuzhou which is approximately 150 miles from the drop off point, and head to the eastern side of the island. Taipei is in the North of the Taiwan island and that area is policed because of the possibilities of a direct attack on the city from the sea.

However, the northeastern coast is deserted,

but the time of travel would need to be timed, so that the landing was staged before the Sun appeared on the horizon.

His spies on the island indicated an area called "Longdong Bay Promontory" was a good landing point. This area is within walking distance of the Dragon Caves. The Dragon Caves have some hidden caves that are used by local tourists, but some caves have not been explored and are sometimes used by the students from the Hemei Elementary or Secondary School. Easy caves might have these kids exploring, but the harder or intermediate caves are left alone both by the adults, children, and the tourists. Wang's people prepared one or two of the caves with some ropes and pulley systems, so that the two Wang personnel: Jian and Helen would be able to get to the caves and lie low for a couple of days. If that failed, they would need an alternative landing site south of the area.

Time of travel depending on the ocean conditions would be 8 to 10 hours using rowing, some quiet engines to get them within five miles of the Promontory. The day after that would be close to the waning moon and would be ideal to stick a landing. Wang was optimistic, but he needed more information from the local spies and the informants and smugglers.

The Coast Guard Administration (CGA), also known as the Taiwan Coast Guard or R.O.C Coast Guard is charged with maintaining law and order and protecting the territorial waters of the Republic of China which surrounds Taiwan, Penghu, Kinmen, Matsu islands, Green Island, Orchid Island, Pratas Island and Nansha Islands. CGA has authority over the waters that surround the various islands of Taiwan and 540,000 Square Kilometers of "Blue Territory" which is fifteen times larger than the island of Taiwan. They have 1 to 16 offshore flotillas which are divided into four sectors. They have a Special Task Unit which is an elite special forces unit of the CGA and their Thunder Squad is likely to be on the lookout for any infiltration from the Chinese secret service or paramilitary forces.

Although the CGA were commissioned on 1 February 2000, They have become very capable and equipped to take on new ocean problems that are targeting Taiwan via sea.

Wang never underestimated the Taiwanese forces. There were too many professionals on both sides of the Taiwan Strait. The mandarins from Mainland were overconfident and were not too concerned with a direct invasion from Taiwan, the Chinese did not monitor their coast like the Taiwanese forces did.

Pottery Making

Knowing that any attempt would result in Helen and Jian taken prisoner and obviously the Taiwanese would play hardball to try to understand what were these two individuals doing in Taiwan? Helen had no flags, but Jian could come up on their radar as a martial arts fighter. Not much to go on, but the Taiwan Intelligence abilities were long and would reach right into Guangdong Province and would track back to the CCP and the MSS. .

Wang gave permission "Let us land them on the weekend, Saturday morning landing at 5:30 am."

The Spies on the island responded with a green light as the place was not active due to the holiday season.

Jian and Helen got dressed for ocean-weather and swimming the last two miles if there were spotted and had to abandon or sink their hovercraft.

Strategy

The one or two person teams were supposed to be the most effective and were able to burrow deep and draw minimum attention.

Medium range was 3 to 10 years and would have the best impact and would involve several two person teams.

If all goes well with this phase, we can start on phase two. However, we must pay attention to the macro scene and not focus on the micro scene. The micro scene or the tension developing in the Taiwan Straits would take precedent and if this escalated, then Wang and the chiefs would have to pause the Taiwan entry and actions beyond the China sea.

The Indo-China situation is quiet, the Asia-Pacific is the macro picture and there are various factors. The COVID crises is subsiding after the five million deaths was reached worldwide. The

2022 January and the winter would determine if the vaccination efforts have gained traction in the Asia-Pacific region. Taiwan has had the best results for vaccination numbers and holding the spread, but that could change. Australia, New Zealand has imposed tight controls and there is a possibility that other Asian countries might have to vaccinate their populations and allow their people to move freely inside and outside their countries.

Supply Chain problems, Inflation fears, Gas prices and various other factors will cause the countries that are dependent on the China movement of supplies to keep the production in various countries flowing.

The year 2022 will be a make-or-break year and it will depend on the supply constraints, vaccination numbers worldwide and the new variants that could suddenly rear their ugly heads and lead to further imposition of border restrictions.

2023 is fast approaching and the Chinese politburo would like to start making a few moves into Taiwan. Mr. Wang and his team were ready for action and were hoping to make a quick attack on Taiwan but were fed up with waiting for the signal from Beijing to come.

Wang wanted to prove that he could make his own move and use his small team and get desired results. He had sent a secret coded message to his boss but had not heard back. The Jian and Helen situation had offered him a quick opportunity to stage a quick attack, but he was worried that if things went wrong, he would be taken to task.

United States

If China invades or occupies Taiwan, Will the United States come to the rescue? That is a very critical question and there is no immediate answer. We do not know, but we can assume that it is not in the interest of the United States to sit and watch as the twenty-four million democratic allies are destroyed and their way of life is changed.

There is a small population of Taiwanese people who secretly are not in favor of the invasion, but there is a subset who would like to have the ability to move and conduct business on the mainland with minimum restrictions.

The environment has been changing. Taiwan is very advanced in chip-making, Artificial Intelligence, Game technology and Internet developments. The social engineering world has changed and Taiwan relates to the rest of the world.

The Chinese on the mainland are isolated and

do not share the democratic values prevalent in Taiwan. The mainland Chinese are capitalists with no democratic movements or social freedoms allowed. China has paramount leader running the show with a large middle class and an upper class of billionaires who have clearance to develop technology and operate with the Chinese monitoring everything that is happening within the country.

The Premier has reversed his liberating policies and is tightening the noose around Chinese entrepreneurs who are getting too big for their boots. The door to grow Chinese industries and build a rich oligarchy is at an end. Most of the big private industries are cautioned to not get ahead of themselves. China would like to rein in all the power and freewheeling and apply restrictions where necessary. Travel for some of these bigwigs has been restricted. Public announcements or interviews to international news reporters is banned outright.

Taiwan is relatively open and does not have any controls on their people and their technology development. All countries in China arena are controlled with very indirect nudging and monitoring by the ruling class.

This long range or remote war has never made the Americans excited about fighting the Chinese.

They will have to move plenty of their naval power and air force to within range of Chinese mainland. Just now, they fly most of their forces from Midway, Hawaii and Alaska.

Taiwan
First Successful Landing

*J*ian and Helen landed on the Northeast Coast of Taiwan. They took shelter in the caves near the cove. There was food and plenty of stuff to keep the wind out and give them rest. If anyone had spotted them coming into the cove, there would be search parties out looking for them.

Jian had been very circumspect and had made sure there was no gear or stuff left on the rocks or floating in the water. The dinghy was sunk in fifteen feet of water and he had a GPS marker in his head as to how to get it back to the surface.

They rested for the night and had alternate lookouts. By morning, there were the usual sounds of the cove area coming alive. Some morning birds, sea birds and usual Taiwanese fishing boats that were blowing their foghorns and going out to sea. Their local people contacted Jian. Wang had instructed them not to wander out until the local guys made contact. They were then transported to a safe house in Taipei, where their papers and their location would be such as to not raise any suspicion. Jian was good at his job and stayed under the radar. They got hold of a few burner phones that they used once a week and from different locations in Taipei. The calls were placed to boats riding on the seas in the Bo Hai bay. Those calls content were relayed to Wang and were very short in duration and basically in simple fisherman's code. The next day, another phone was used to relay a message that was just touch points and just to keep Wang feeling comfortable about their situation.

The Coastguard, the Naval force and the military were not in any alert status, Wang was therefore confident that his guys had slipped in. The coast was clear and no reason to get excited. Phase 2 of their attack should be put in motion. Wang and Jian decided to let a few days go by. Wang would give the go ahead for the attack date and their plan would be set in motion.

Helen and Jian tried to keep a low profile. Minimize any contact with the locals. Eat the usual food and stay away from any of the bars and night scene. Helen was instructed to not make any unnecessary contact with Taiwanese or other people. Keep things simple.

Helen Tsai
Runs into Trouble

The Wop Tu Triad catches up with Helen Tsai. It was an accident as Helen was not very circumspect in her dealings with civilians. She tended to trust foreign persons of Chinese origin. She saw the good in them and sometimes did not see the jealousy or bad that was hidden beneath their conversations. She was not casual in her dealings and just kept to herself.

She was out to get the groceries and even though she had been warned by Jian not to engage in conversations with any unknown persons and especially with any Cantonese or Mandarin speaking individuals. There were likely to be questions and she would stumble and blow their cover.

Helen was in a casual exchange with a shopper who was supposed to be from Singapore. She made contact and failed to report back to Jian. The information started to get back to the triads and within a day or two the Wop Tu were sniffing in the area. The Wop Tu had lost interest and believed the trail was cold and that the two persons had fled the mainland, Hong Kong and were headed to a distant foreign country.

However, Jian noticed that there were a couple of persons who seemed to be idling around their accommodations. He never used the same route and sometimes even retraced his steps, which is when he caught sight of the two guys who were following Helen Tsai but at a safe distance. This was not good.

"What did these guys want with her?"

"Or were they just following orders from some Triad Chief?"

"If I do not neutralize these guys, Helen will be in trouble."

Jian was breathing slowly and just tailed the guys to comprehend their motives.

That evening he questioned Helen about these strange guys on her tail. Helen confessed that she had gotten friendly with a Chinese expatriate who was from the islands. She assumed that it was not a problem. Jian assured her that the island person must have talked to someone and the information got back to their enemies in China or maybe Hong

Kong. The Wop Tu were always looking out for them, but not actively. However, they did not let sleeping dogs lie.

Jian reported this to his handler: Mr. Wang. Wang started to query the underworld and see if he could produce any information about the shadows and their sudden interest in Jian and Helen.

The following evening, when Helen was getting back from her gym, she was accosted by a couple of thugs of varied sizes and shapes. Helen looked around for help and speed dialed Jian. Her phone was transmitting the event as it was happening. Jian picked up and listened to what was going down.

"Do you want to have some fun, pretty lady?" one of the roughnecks probed her.

She kept her cool and did not respond but slowly made it to a well-lit part of the street.

"You do not want to join us at a party or maybe a bar?" another guy reached and grabbed her from behind.

She tried to ward him off and failed to see the blow that he directed at the side of her head.

She went down without a sound and realized that she was not able to defend herself any longer. She curled into a ball and started to scream hoping to attract attention and scare these idiots who were up to no good.

The five guys started to kick her. The kicks landed on her back, her head, and her stomach. Street thugs are trained to beat up anybody and reduce them to mush.

These guys were professionals and had boots that really hurt. The speed of the kicks increased in intensity, and she started to see black and then passed out. Before she passed out, she needed to at least give them the impression that she would come back to haunt their dreams.

Jian was running and trying to get to the location where he thought Helen would be on the street bleeding and losing her life. He called for help and gave an approximate location for the beating.

"The WOP TU or its proxies were taking care of business. They beat Helen and she was dead by now."

Jian was shaken as he pondered the situation.

When Jian got to the street, he saw Helen's body lying on the street in a pool of blood and he assumed the worst. When he touched her body on the ground, there was a faint pulse, and she was fighting for her life. She was making some strange sounds and was in shock. He had to carry her, get her to safety.

He started to whisper to her: "please stay awake and do not fall asleep. I will get you to a hospital and safety."

She started to mutter something, " I am sorry. I got you in trouble. Please forgive me. " And then she passed out.

The ambulance arrived, followed by a police car. The techs applied all sorts of medical bandages and salve to her visible wounds. They gave her breathing apparatus and were busy monitoring her vitals. They called ahead to the hospital. The rest would be addressed at the hospital. They loaded her on a stretcher and started to drive her to the nearest emergency center. He queried the driver, and they indicated a place that was less than a mile of two away. He got there before the ambulance and he waited as they pulled in.

No Wop Tu in sight or their compatriots who gave Helen the beating. Obviously, they were long gone. The cowards would beat up a lady who had no intent to cause them harm.

Jian rushed into the hospital, but he did not have to worry, Helen was taken care of and although it was touch and go, she would live and get past this.

The beating had left the body battered beyond recognition. There were marks on her hands as she tried to ward off blows, but eventually she succumbed to the beating and was unconscious as they continued to kick her in the head and neck areas.

The face, neck, and skull were partially protected by her hands and eventually, she received the brunt of their kicks to her back, abdomen, hands, and legs. The abrasions to her body and abdomen would scar her for life. She would need exceptional care and facial surgery to become whole again. Internal bleeding and even damage to her internal organs would probably heal if treated by professional doctors.

The trauma is always too much for a lady like Helen, but the intensity of the attack and the violence of the attack was too much. The concussion and trauma were already causing swelling of her head and neck and there would be complications once the internal bleeding had stopped.

The Professional Taiwanese doctors were phenomenal in their treatment of Helen since they were trained in the United States and were used to treating war time injuries which were ten times worse.

"If only I could get my hands on these idiots." Jian said to himself.

"Somebody will have to pay for this." He continued. Jian was mad and he was beside himself with grief.

He was talking to himself and screaming obscenities at the wall.

He punched the wall and started to murmur about the crazy people kicking Helen. In between, he called Helen all sorts of nasty names for blowing their cover.

He was not sure if he would be able to identify this group's leader.

The pursuit of these thugs would not be easy and he would end up dead or worse still maimed like Helen.

He needed to be smart and calm. He talked to Mr. Wang and got his guidance on the matter.

Wang knew that this had really affected Jian Wu's thinking and it would not be easy for him to concentrate on what needs to be done.

"So, Plan B would be initiated and triggered from Xiamen."

Wang gave instructions "Move Helen to a safe location in Taiwan; monitor her 24/7 until she is well and able to take care of herself."

Wang's strict orders to Jian:

"Do not even attempt to go see her or find her."

Jian did not take this well, but he realized it was for Helen's and his survival.

Meanwhile. Susie Wong and her team were informed of what transpired in Taiwan and they were asked to proceed to move some of their team into Taiwan and Taipei. Stage another team landing on the coast. Wang talked to Susie's handler and the die was cast that Susie and her sidekick or woman would make the second landing.

Wang needed to get explosives and M16 carbines, AK47 and sufficient bullets to start a minor attack. Things had not gone well and the team needed additional help and more firepower to stage an attack and achieve success. Leave nothing to chance.

To divert the Taiwanese attention from the second landing, Wang advised his counter group to stage some activities near the Pratas Islands. These Chinese intrusions into the Pratas Islands in the South China Sea, which was part of Cijin District, Kaohsiung, Republic of China, Taiwan.

The Pratas islands are 530 miles south of Taipei. These islands are relatively far away from what was occurring near Northern Eastern Taipei, but Wang knew that this would keep the Taiwanese from paying attention to what was happening in the North. The distraction had to be staged in such a way as to divert all attention from the capital city of Taipei and the oceanside where the team was setting up to be operational.

Susie and her compatriot Miso were taken on

a SeaRey special aircraft that is quiet and could get them close to the general area that Jian and Helen landed in the northeast. They needed equipment and guns to be dropped nearby and they needed to retrieve these weapons. They chose a night that was stormy compared to a moonless night. They landed out at sea and were able to use small handheld motors to bring them into the coast. Most of this was done in scuba outfit underwater. Jian was there to receive them. The guns and ammunition along with explosives would be retrieved by their team on a separate night. All the equipment was tested and sealed from the saltwater before dumping it underwater. It would be very serious to give a defective piece of fighting equipment to a fighter. This would be death in a foreign country.

The sea was choppy and they made it into the bay without too much of drama. Jian and Susie talked for the first time in many years. Miso stayed in the background and listened to their chatter. She was trained to listen and not get in the way. Jian's mates would have to pick up the guns and ammunition from the ocean. They had the drop points and the guns were safe and insulated from the seawater and were sunk in about sixty feet of water.

Jian needed to make sure that the guns and

equipment were picked up from the Lat-Long. location Where they were dropped. Jian and Susie went to the cave and after a few hours of quiet chat, they fell asleep.

Susie and Miso were fast asleep as they were exhausted with the whole ocean journey.

Jian stayed wide awake and looked at the night sky through the cave opening. He was pondering about Helen and wondering how she was doing. The drugs and the antibiotics would do their magic. The Taiwanese doctors were very competent in their use of western and eastern medicine and used all their training to bring Helen back to the land of the living.

There was going to be several weeks of healing and rehab before she would be able to get out of bed and be able to possibly lead a normal life.

Attack Begins

The next day the "Go Ahead" message came through. Jian and his team of six locals, Susie and Miso were asked to proceed to City Hall area in Taipei.

Jian and Susie were quite excited. Their adrenaline pumping and their hearts beating at a rapid clip, they were ready to knock out the City Hall's defenses. They retrieved the sunken guns, explosives, and ammunition. They needed to position themselves close to the target that they were going to attack near City Hall. The building on 120 Songkran Road was a staging place for the Taiwan military Rapid Response team in Taipei. It was across from the Meridien Hotel and looked very ordinary like a shopping mall. The Shopping mall had been closed for quite some time. It was operating at 50% capacity and was more of a façade. The Military or RRT had a separate entrance to the building via the underground. It was not visible from the street, but it is believed that there are about 500-to-1000-man/women armed team that could roll out of there. This crack force was not aware of the attack that was coming their way.

Jian and his team would hit the building with the full force of explosions and heavy fire. Once they got into the building, they would take over the control room and see what these troops were looking at. Total time of entry and departure without too much delay was 1 hour to neutralize the forces, then move to the Night market district near the Tamsui River.

There would be a fast boat to take them up the river to the entrance. If they got there without too much hassle, the Chinese would position a submarine that would take them out to sea. This total operation was expected to take a maximum of 2 hours from start to finish. However, everything would have to go with clockwork and there should not be too much of awareness in the first two hours from the local police, the military, or the special forces.

If it exceeded this 2-hour time limit, then all bets were off and there would be a lot of Taiwanese forces heading in their general direction. The force against them would be huge and there would be no chance of their escape from the great island of Taiwan.

Time of attack was set for early morning. The streets were empty. The guards were changing and alert levels would be usually low. Most attacks take place just a few minutes before dawn. Jian and his team using two separate cars were enroute to the place at a little before 5 am. The streets were empty, but life was starting. Sounds of traffic were building up. The underground had already started its continuous service, but the number of early riders was still miniscule. The attack time was approaching and the team was all ready to go.

Jian asked the team to synchronize their watches as the attack time was set for 6:10 am. At about 8:10 am, they were expected to be at the night market bridge headed for the open sea. If that did not work, they would have to speed up the exit from the city. The advance team got to the entrance, where they applied the plastic explosives to the door. The explosion was light but could be heard across the street. Once the doors were blown open, the team made a quick entrance. Nobody was there to greet them.

They proceeded quickly and after a quick scan, they saw a group of people in plainclothes but with small caliber pistols and sidearms. His team took them out and proceeded into the next room. With their suppressed automatics, they were able to rapidly control the floor. There were no radio sounds, so the team was probably several floors above. They took the stairs quickly and proceeded to the upper floors.

Susie and the other team were taking the North stairs, while Jian, Miso and his 3-man team went up the south stairs. They were up at the fourth floor, where they met small arms fire. They continued until the shooting from upper floors got more intense. Jian proceeded to hear footfalls and decided to proceed with caution. On that floor, there was a contingent of soldiers who were trained, armed and ready. Not expecting too much of opposition, they fired and cleared the floors to get to the control floor which was on the fourth floor.

Here there were the other soldiers waiting to engage the intruders. He called his North team and found that they were at the fourth floor and using explosives had entered the control room. They engaged and took down several of the staff. Some they tied up with quick plastic ties. The rest they knocked unconscious.

Jian and Miso split up and ran up the floors to the control floor. They entered this area rapidly and faced very little opposition. Jian took over and checked all the monitors and entrances. Less than 8 minutes since their breech of the building entrance.

"Where were the soldiers? Nobody in sight." Muttered Jian under his breath.

The monitors did not give them much help as the entrances to the building did not show any persons entering or leaving. He called Wang and updated him on the special coded handsets they carried with them. The Taiwanese troops were somewhere in the building, in the basement and unaware that the building was breached on the street level.

"You have another 30 minutes to finish the job. If you do not complete it, move on, and get to the Night market."

"Should we abort the mission as we face no opposition. Proceed to Phase 2 and destroy all the computers, camera monitoring equipment and move on."

"Go ahead and do what we came to do. You will have a tough passage to the sea, so exit early like in 20 minutes."

This was really disconcerting and Jian was not wanting to hang out any longer.

"Destroy all the equipment and exit the building in 10 minutes. Let us meet on the streets and take the cars to the Night Street market bridge."

Pottery Making

Susie did not meet any opposition on the other side of the building, but she proceeded to take her team to the basement. There she met several armed soldiers who were waiting for them. The automatic fire was very orchestrated and direct and two of her team got hit even with Kevlar protection. Susie used explosive and flash bangs. The explosions were loud and the noise was alarming and distinct. She and the other guy exchanged a fast spray of bullets to wipe out the persons behind that first door. The next room, they cleared very rapidly.

She called Jian to find out how he was doing and gave him a quick summary of the events in the basement. She even added that two of her team were injured and they needed to evacuate, before they bled to death. Jian and his team reached the basement by 6:25am. They proceeded to clear the floor. There were no injuries as they added to their team's fire power.

At 6:30 am, They hobbled out of the building. Susie worked on one of her men and reduced the blood flow. The other man's injury needed more attention, so she put a tourniquet. They got into the cars and sped back to the night market bridge. Here they were surprised to find that there were people on the streets cleaning and getting in their way. They spent a few minutes before they spotted the speed boats. There was the smiling captain. They jumped in to the first speed boat. Susie and her team assisted the wounded soldiers onto the other speed boat. They took off at about 6:45 am.

They made good time. Now for the sea. They had to go under two bridges. There was no trouble under bridge one. As they neared bridge two, rapid fire hit the boat. This was to sink them. Susie returned fire and the gun stopped as suddenly as it started. No missiles were used. Just automatic and small arms fire.

They were under the second bridge, when a missile came and blasted near one of their boats. The fight was getting very close. They reached the open sea. The coast guard had been informed and were racing to this place with heavy armaments. They sped out to sea, but their speed dropped as the ocean currents and waves slowed them down to about ten knots per hour. Jian was upset that their twenty-five knots per hour speedboats were not making any progress.

Where was Wang and his submarine. No friend in sight. On the horizon, there were two Coast Guard vessels speeding towards them. They would be on them at about 7:12 am. Time to die, if we do not do something. After a mile or so as Taipei was receding in the distance, they suddenly saw the submarine surface about five miles in front of them. This was touch and go.

They increased their speed and were now bobbing on the waves at about twenty knots per hour. They would just make it to the submarine as the Coast Guard would get to them. Jian and Susie looked at each other across the Taipei Ocean. They knew that this was going to be extremely close for comfort. They were about two miles from the sub and the sub was also moving towards them. The sub fired a couple of torpedoes at the approaching CG vessels, The two vessels started to apply some avoidance maneuvers and throw some dummy torpedoes at the armed ones.

Jian and his teams arrived at the submarine. They got assistance from the sub crew to board the injured personnel. As they continued to bring in Jian, Susie and Miso, there were new dangers on the horizons. Two jets were approaching on their bombing runs to take out the submarine. The commander gave the signal to dive and the rest of the crew were hurried on board. In less than a minute, the submarine took off and turned. The jet flew by and threw a few depth charges.

The submarine had not reached diving depth but was leaving the area fast.

The speed at which they took off impressed

the Taiwanese Air Force. This was not good. The Chinese sent us a message.

We need to be always alert. An invasion is imminent.

Taiwanese Military Response

It appears that the Taiwanese military is aware of China's intentions and needs to be wary and careful. We need more assistance from the Western powers especially America. When the assault takes place, it will be an all-out war and we do not stand a chance against the Chinese military machinery.

We must retaliate now. The Taiwanese brass and the government met at the highest level and were studying their next moves. It appears that we were in a very vulnerable place. The Chinese spies have infiltrated our lands and are all over the island especially in Taipei, the capital city. We must understand that this is not a mere exercise. This is real in 2021. By 2022, China will send their invasion force and there will be a repeat of 1950 and 1951, when the Mainland Chinese bombed us for many days and continued to decimate the Taiwanese defenses.

The People's Republic of China is now an advanced military force and their military abilities have come a long way from their 1970s capabilities. Their past wars with Vietnam and Taiwan are not indicative of what is coming Taiwan's way in 2022 or beyond.

Taiwan goes to a Code Red: All their forces are on high alert. All personnel are ready to defend the island nation. All the military, air force and Naval forces are ready to defend island and attack the mainland of China. If the PRC decides to use their armed forces to attack our island, there will be a huge price to pay. Taiwan armed forces, Air Force and Military are working with the United States seventh fleet, and the other military Western forces in the Pacific and the South China sea.

Recovery

Mr. Jian and his compatriots are back in Xiamen, PRC, and the condition of the combatants after the attack is serious, they need at least two to three weeks of recovery and rehab. The setback that the Taiwanese Military has faced in their capital city, Taipei was quite serious and they are trying to understand how it happened and what total losses they suffered.

Mr. Wang of the MSS, PRC does not believe that they have time to prepare for another MSS attack on the island. They will have to allow the Chinese naval forces, air force, and military to come up with an invasion date and proceed to the attack around the Chinese new year in February.

The Taiwanese Military brass will be expecting it and will go on a wartime defensive effort.

The Americans are starting to move their Naval vessels and other Military into the Pacific Bases in Guam, Midway, Alaska. Radio chatter has increased in the South China sea and in the Pacific Ocean. Some naval and aircraft are heading to the south and will be positioned for a complete defense of Taiwan or assault on mainland China. The question was: "Who was going to blink first?"

The Taiwanese Military is being cautioned by the Republic of China Central Authority in Taipei not to declare an all-out war with the Chinese Military but stage an attack on Xiamen or Shanghai. "An eye for an eye, limited engagement."

Focus on Military targets, not Civilian like the Russians in Ukraine.

There are senior military officers who believe that the Chinese military is wanting a war on all fronts. They do not care about the consequences. They just worry that their people need this war to unite the Mainland Chinese people.

Finally, it is agreed that a very limited attack on Xiamen would give the Mainland Chinese the retaliation that is required to send the message to Beijing. If they do not get it, then we might have to take it to the next level. An Attack on Shanghai or Fuzhou: Shanghai has too many people and no military offensive weapons. Fuzhou has a couple of missile batteries that are directed at Taipei. This is approximately 158 aerial miles and can be done with a couple of quick sorties across the bay.

Final Battle

The attack on Xiamen, Eastern China began the very next day at 05:00 am in the morning. The F15 and F16 stay low over the horizon and attack the major PRC naval base that is prepared for an attack but did not expect one this early. The planes come in low over the horizon and drop bombs and missiles that destroy much of the infrastructure of the base. The number of civilians killed were low and there were several military personnel who were killed or injured.

The airplanes dropped their missiles and bombs and flew back to their bases. The attack took about 20 to 30 minutes. The Chinese military was on high alert and the command structure in Beijing realized what happened and decided to escalate to the top brass who in turn escalated to the Paramount leader: Mr. Xi Jinping.

Mr. Xi was very upset with this whole sequence of events. He had worked through the ranks in Fujian Province. He met the well-known folksinger Peng Liyuan and married her in 1987. He worked his way up to deputy provincial party secretary. In 1999, he became acting governor of Fujian and governor the following year. He had worked for cooperation with Taiwan.

This was a direct attack on him. He had worked his way up in Shanghai and Xiamen and was very committed to the unification of China and Taiwan. This sequence of attacks by the MSS, PRC and followed by Taiwanese airplanes told him that the PRC could escalate to an all-out war and the ending would not be pretty as it would draw other forces into the conflict.

Xi's Backstory

Though his father and he had suffered after the Tiananmen massacre, His father was severally reprimanded, and Xi was sent into 6 years of reeducation and was knocked out of running for the Politburo. His fortunes changed as he worked his way up and accepted tough positions. His major role was cleaning up corruption in China.

He asked his Military to have a very high-level meeting with him and his inner core. The meeting was held at 9:00 am. That day. Xi realized if action was not taken, the Taiwanese would think he was afraid to have an open war or conflict with Taiwan. The Americans would probably be dragged in and the war would not be good for the two powers and the rest of Asia.

The last time a war was waged in this part of the world in 1951, the Americans threatened to use nuclear weapons on the Chinese people near Taiwan. With Biden in command and the American people tired of war, this would be the perfect time for China to go to war.

Invasion of Taiwan should be their main objective and should be accomplished before Christmas 2023.

By 10:30 am, the Americans were informed about the attack on Xiamen Naval base and its destruction by the Taiwanese airplanes. The Americans were starting to realize that this was going to escalate to an all-out war between the two countries. Biden sent his top cabinet personnel to Beijing to have a cautious engagement and de-escalate or this would result in an all-out war on the continent.

The Chinese Paramount Leader and the American President were on the phone and although the discussion was amicable, The Chinese Leader was under duress and would have to respond to the Taiwanese attack. The US President understood the extent of the temperature rise, but he was a man of extreme caution. The Chinese Premier was wanting to wage war on Taiwan and take it by force now that the time for niceties has passed. He did not want to appear to be a weak leader.

The American President called the President of Taiwan on the hot line. The discussion was not very amicable as the lady president was angry about the low-level Chinese PRC attack on their Capital City, Taipei. She was not calm about the way it was done and the number of people who were killed because of that attack.

The UN was having the Security meeting about this new situation and they passed a few resolutions to ask both China and Taiwan ROC to conduct a cease fire before this got out of hand. The UN realized it was a tit-for-tat and that there was damage, death, and destruction on both sides, but the chance for peace was within the hands of the Beijing and Taipei's leaders.

The American Secretary of State and the US Defense Secretary flew to Taipei. it was now or never. The two nations were going to war and it would be a bloodbath.

TRANSFORMATION

Jian and Wang were called to Beijing for an immediate meeting with the great leader. Wang was stressed out as they made the Air Force flight to the Capital City.

Wang was so tensed up that Jian was afraid to ask him anything.

"How is this going to end?" muttered Jian under his breath.

Wang was non-committal. He just did not want to make any conversation.

Stuff was going through his mind and he was expecting a demotion, probably a few years in Daquing for re-education. Or worse still a bullet through his brain.

"I should receive a medal of valor or honor" were his thoughts.

"However, one did not know what to expect from the bigwigs."

The Chiefs in an autocratic society were mad if you did and mad if you did not.

Original thinking was not encouraged especially if you got egg on the PRC's face.

They arrived in Beijing in the late evening. Jian was starting to get very pensive and was tapping his feet towards the end. Wang had very bad premonition that this was not good for Jian or the team.

They were met by the security guards and checked for even pens and pencils. They met with the right-hand man of Xi and no questions were asked or answered, but a stern warning not to interrupt Xi as he was in a very bad mood.

"Stop Fidgeting" He warned Jian and asked them to keep their head and eyes looking at Xi. "Answer only if questions are directed at you"

The door was open and the two marched towards the Premier.

"Attention and Relax, but do not sit down!!!"

The Premier started: "It is obvious you have taken initiative, without consulting with your boss or anyone and the results are going to be very bad for the PRC."

"Usually, the consequences for this are death or imprisonment for the rest of your sorry lives. Your family and friends will never know what happened to you as you will be buried side by side in unmarked graves or even burned beyond recognition."

"Do you have anything to say for yourselves?"

Mr. Xi raised his voice and continued in a guttural voice like a school master or a prison administrator.

"You have made the PRC and I lose face in front of the world. I have spent 10 years of my life building a relationship with Taiwan from my last two positions in Shanghai and Fujian province. Now it is ALL ERASED!!! There is no going back.

The Taiwanese and the Americans are ready to break down our doors and subdue us with heavy attacks from the sea, land, and air. You have no idea of the damage that you have done. Do you?"

Wang started to shiver and shake. Jian was close to collapsing next to him.

"Guards" The Premier spat on the ground

The doors opened and Mr. Wang was accosted out of the room.

He was handcuffed and blindfolded.

Jian was standing untouched while this was going on. He did not even dare raise his eyes or move a muscle.

"Take two steps forward and pay close attention.

You will now report directly to me.

You will check with me for everything you do.

Even to breathe, you will ask permission. Your team will report to you directly and I want you to know that all this will blow over and I will send you my instructions in the next couple of days or weeks.

Stay in Beijing and await my orders. Got it."

The End